THE
BEGGAR
PRINCE

ONCE UPON A PRINCE

onceuponaprinceseries.com

KATE STRADLING

THE BEGGAR PRINCE

ONCE UPON A PRINCE

A KING THRUSHBEARD RETELLING

THE BEGGAR PRINCE

This is a work of fiction. Names, characters, places, organizations, and events are either the product of the author's imagination or are used in a fictitious manner.

Cover art by MoorBooks Design

Published by
Eulalia Skye Press
P.O. Box 2203, Mesa, AZ 85214
eulaliaskye.com

ISBN: 978-1-947495-17-3

For Darrell,
who will likely never read this
(Which is fine. He's cool anyway.)

CHAPTER 1

We're not actually going to this thing, are we?" Thorben of Hauke angled in his saddle for a better glimpse of the road. Past the thinning pines, black stone walls loomed, soldiers impeding traffic through huge gates as they checked carts and saddlebags. Beyond, the city of Felstark hummed with life beneath a pale morning sun.

Its castle, crowning the mountain apex, jutted in the distance. He hadn't seen it in over a decade and wouldn't care if he never saw it again.

"This *thing*?" A gray gelding joined his chestnut, the pair of horses abreast as the second rider eyed him. "This *thing* is the only reason your mother allowed you out of your castle. I thought you promised her you'd go."

"I promised I'd come to Felstark, Marco. I said nothing about my activities here."

"Foul play, Tor," a voice called behind them. Thorben twisted to arch a brow at his younger brother, but Berthold merely arched his own brows back. "You know Mother thought we were going. She'll ask about it when we get home. Besides, don't you want to see the Laughing Princess?"

"No," said Thorben flatly. He'd met Leonie more than a decade ago during a state visit to Elisia, and that one encounter had been enough for a lifetime. The snobbish creature had stared at him for fully a minute, and when he finally looked back, she'd turned away and never glanced at him again.

She wasn't even her kingdom's heir, and she'd acted like its queen. At the time, her mother had made excuses about her being shy, but shyness didn't explain the initial stare. For whatever reason, Princess Leonie had deemed him beneath her touch. He'd resolved to mirror that courtesy for the rest of his life.

And besides that, everyone in this country had pronounced his name wrong, and he was fairly certain they'd done it on purpose.

"They spell their version without the h," his father had said at the time, excusing the offense as a minor faux pas. "You can't blame them for pronouncing yours how it looks to them."

But he could. Twelve kingdoms across the central Nivean Mountains all spoke the same language—admittedly with variation—but only Elisia had developed a lisp where his name was concerned. He'd spent a very unpleasant week correcting everyone who addressed him, all while they chuckled and cosseted him like he was a baby.

Meanwhile, the only other person near his age had pretended that he didn't exist.

"She's an angel," a dreamy voice intoned. All eyes shifted to the speaker, Alois of Arbenia, who seemed taken in a trance as his horse plodded along.

"Didn't she call you a dullard during your last visit?" Marco bluntly asked.

A faint blush arose on the other young man's cheeks, his posture stiffening. "It wasn't what she said, but how she said it, with her smiling eyes and her sparkling, musical laugh."

The pair at the front of the group exchanged a glance. In Thorben's experience, laughter enhanced an insult rather than disarming it, but Alois was obviously a lost cause where the Princess of Elisia was concerned.

"We have to go, Tor," said Marco with a shrug. "Not only because your mother will question you and Bert, but because she'll question *me*, and I don't want to run afoul of her."

Thorben, unwilling to concede, tipped his head. "But if we send Alois by himself, aren't his chances better?"

"Highly doubtful," Marco muttered, too low for the Prince of Arbenia to hear.

A derisive huff escaped Thorben before he could stop it. "Whoever heard of letting a princess pick her husband from a crowd? The whole event is crude."

"I don't think we're in any danger."

"I'm certainly not," Berthold chirped, earning himself another dour glance from his older brother. At seventeen, the younger prince barely qualified as a marriage candidate in his own kingdom, let alone for a foreign princess. Marco, merely the son of a Haukien duke, would merit less notice than most of the Elisian nobles who answered their king's invitation. Alois, like Berthold, was a prince but a second son, unlikely to inherit the throne of Arbenia thanks to an older brother who had already wed and sired an heir.

Thorben, though, was mere weeks from becoming king, already regarded as one by most of his subjects. If Leonie was concerned only for rank in her marriage alliance, he might be her most alluring choice.

If she chose. Rumor whispered that the contrary princess had sworn to a life of solitude and celibacy, which nicely explained why she kept mocking her suitors back out the doors they entered.

He wasn't keen on trusting rumors, though.

"Elisia's an important ally," Marco said, chiding in his voice. "Their silver mines are second to none, and we need their iron unless you want to strengthen ties with Beroa."

A muscle rippled along Thorben's jaw. He raised his eyes to the lofty pines, whose needles swayed in the summer breeze. The walls of Felstark hid all but the highest castle tower from view now.

Marco persisted. "How long can it possibly take? We have to stay here overnight anyway. We can stop in at the choosing for half an hour, come home, sleep, and continue on our way at dawn."

If only he'd delayed his departure another day. But then his mother wouldn't have allowed him to come at all. Queen Julika, acting as his regent, had been loath enough for him to leave Swifthaven with his coronation date so near. She certainly wouldn't have countenanced a mere hunting excursion among friends, not without confining him to Hauke and appending a whole platoon of guards to dog his every step.

He wanted one last taste of *freedom* before he dedicated the rest of his life to his people. He didn't regret his future, but no one had planned for him to inherit so soon. Certainly he had not anticipated gaining a crown the same day he gained his majority.

Twenty-one was too young. His father should have lived another three decades, into hoary old age instead of dying in his prime.

But Thorben's youth underscored the need to reinforce political alliances. Hauke and Elisia had not always been on good terms. One evening in Felstark's castle could strengthen ties that frayed far too easily.

Leonie had considered him beneath notice when they were children. Chances were she would feel the same now that they were both grown.

His hands tightened around his reins, leather gloves taut across his knuckles. "Half an hour," he said with an unhappy grunt.

Marco allowed his horse to lag, though not before Thorben saw the smugness that tugged at the corners of his mouth.

Insufferable. His recent appointment to the king's council was going to his head.

As they drew near Felstark's tall western gate, a spotted mare cantered to the front of their group. Thorben's valet, Gereon, who had remained with their other servants and supply horses, now nodded to his king and preceded him, the first to intercept the Elisian soldiers.

They took one glance at his livery, at the royal crest of Hauke emblazoned on his suit's left breast, and waved the whole company through with no further inspection. Four nobles, eight guards and servants, and two additional pack horses passed into the teeming city. Smells of the west market assaulted them, savory herbs and frying oil, with fruits and vegetables like jewels lining carts and stalls. The crush of bodies and carriages slowed their progress. Further on, when shops replaced the open-air exchange, the street widened. Thorben, with no memory of how to navigate this foreign city, followed his valet.

Soon, Alois joined him. "You're staying at your embassy?"

Thorben nodded. "You're welcome to camp there with us."

He puffed his chest importantly. "King Eustis said I could have rooms in the royal wing." As he'd mentioned this every other hour since he'd joined them at the crossroads, the declaration failed to impress.

"You're still hunting with us tomorrow, though?"

"Oh, of course. Wouldn't miss it."

"Even if you end this evening betrothed?" Thorben wryly asked.

A wrinkle marred Alois's forehead, his eyes going vacant. "I'm sure Leonie wouldn't mind. It's not as though the wedding would be immediate, and hunting in Elisia trumps hunting anywhere else. Perhaps she'll want to come—"

"*No.*" Thorben wore such a withering expression that his fellow royal cringed. "If she comes, so does her maid and a cook and no doubt half a dozen other attendants. This was supposed to be a small, *informal* hunt among friends."

"I'll bring her back a stag's antlers as a gift," Alois said, as though this would make up for abandoning a woman he wasn't even betrothed to yet, and who seemed not to favor him at all.

Perhaps he really was a dullard. Thorben sighed and lapsed back into his own thoughts. The nearer they drew to the castle, the nicer their surroundings became. At last, the Prince of Arbenia parted ways, leaving the delegation from Hauke to continue on the main road.

"I forgot he's so insufferable when he's besotted," Marco said, watching over his shoulder as Alois, a stiff valet, and two Arbenish guards disappeared among a press of carriages.

"How long has he been courting Leonie?" Thorben asked.

"I think King Eustis began inviting suitors the moment she turned eighteen. I'm fairly certain you received two or three gilt-edged letters yourself before your father died."

He stilled, casting his thoughts backward. Weeks of wasting illness and the months that followed had consumed his memories of life before that drastic change. "I think I did," he finally concluded.

"You threw them away," said Marco knowingly.

"No. Gereon would have answered them with a polite excuse for my absence, and then *he* would have thrown them away. But that means this started almost two years ago. Has she really been staving off every man who appeared for so long?"

His advisor shrugged. "Maybe the one she wanted never showed up."

Only a fool would have missed his implied meaning. Thorben scoffed. "Maybe she's really taken an oath of celibacy. Regardless, it's none of my business."

Up ahead, his valet had dismounted beside a gate in the wall that lined this street. Gereon pulled the bell and briefly conversed with a guard on the other side. As the portal opened wide, Thorben breathed deep.

It was his first visit to Elisia as a king. His ambassadors and diplomats stationed here—appointed by his father—would ingratiate themselves in a push to keep their post or gain a more prestigious one. Hence, he would have preferred avoiding Felstark altogether.

The embassy was by far preferable to the castle, though. He steeled himself for the necessary back-and-forth, for the offers from diplomats to join his entourage tonight, from the inevitable compliments they would pay both to him and to the marriageable princess he supposedly came to court.

She should have chosen someone in the past year, while he could still claim his mourning as an excuse not to come. Instead, she had meticulously ridiculed all her suitors, thus driving her father to drastic measures.

Princess Leonie of Elisia still thought herself above every other creature in the world, and Thorben of Hauke wanted nothing to do with her. After tonight, he would continue to his appointed hunting lodge and forget she'd ever existed.

CHAPTER 2

Thorben survived the gauntlet of embassy diplomats and spent the afternoon in his valet's care. Meticulous to a fault, Gereon eliminated all traces of dust and travel from his royal charge. Hours later, the not-yet-crowned King of Hauke departed for Felstark Castle with nary a thread out of place on his person, impatient for an end to his evening before it ever began.

King Eustis greeted the Haukien delegation himself, grasping Thorben's hands the moment he stepped into the castle's reception room. "A delight to have you here again, young man. It has been far too long." This sentiment might have held more weight had he not lisped the initial consonant of the young king's name when he introduced him to the Elisian dignitaries beside him.

"Simon, you remember Thorben of Hauke."

Simon, Duke of Ursinbau, inclined his head, a frown puckering his lips. "Well met, Your Majesty." Thorben vaguely recalled him from that ill-fated visit more than a decade ago. In a kingdom that prohibited female heirs, the duke was next in line for the

Elisian throne. "May I present my wife Naira and our eldest, Dyrk." The woman at his side dipped into a deep curtsey. A bejeweled escoffion hid her hair from sight, its green silk matching the velvet of her dress to a shade. At her throat, an emerald brooch winked in the candlelight. Her son, not even in his teens yet, bowed. His presence among the crowd of adults touched Thorben's sympathies. The boy looked bored out of his skull.

"And here we have the Baroness Amelise Rotholt," said King Eustis. The curiously indulgent twist in his voice reminded Thorben of the sound an overstuffed cushion made when sat upon. He glanced at the purple-clad woman in deep curtsey—the glittering escoffion that matched her gown, glimpses of snowy white fabric at her collar and sleeves—before returning his attention to the Elisian king.

Eustis was a widower, his wife having passed seven years prior. From the way he observed the baroness, though, he did not intend to remain alone much longer. Though her headdress marked her as a married woman, no baron stood beside her, and the king regarded her with eyes that would make any husband bristle.

She was young—certainly young enough to bear him a true heir. The Duke and Duchess of Ursinbau remained aloof as though oblivious to the coy atmosphere between king and baroness. Thorben, keen to avoid unnecessary political intrigue, dragged his brother forward to complete the introductions.

He very carefully pronounced the hard consonant that sat at the center of Bert's given name. "I've brought Prince Berthold with me. It's his first time in your superb country."

The King of Elisia inclined his head, and his speculative gaze swept the younger man from head to toe. "How thoughtful. I'm sure Leonie will be glad to meet you as well."

"Is the princess not here yet?" Bert asked, his youth allowing such a bald question as he glanced around the company assembled further in the room. "I've heard she's the most beautiful woman in the Twelve Kingdoms." Indeed, Alois had regaled them with this information for half their journey here.

King Eustis chuckled, but the baroness's smile grew brittle. "Yes, Leonie is quite a wonder," she said, forced courtesy dripping from her words.

Perhaps the haughty princess wasn't ready for a stepmother. Perhaps the would-be stepmother was reluctant to dwell alongside such a jewel. Thorben, determined to let these familial woes play out as far from him as possible, plastered on his most pleasant smile. "We'll be happy to greet her as well when she appears." So saying, he guided his brother further into the room, leaving behind the king and company to acknowledge their next set of guests.

Bert elbowed his stiff-backed older brother as they walked. "She's not even here. Maybe you can pass your half-hour without ever meeting her."

"I could be so lucky."

The younger prince alone had received his full confidence, which had piqued Bert's interest in the so-called Laughing Princess all the more.

"It sounds like King Eustis expects you to participate in the choosing," said Thorben, a warning in his voice. "You could end this night with a betrothal."

Bert's good cheer did not dampen in the least. "That would be fun to explain to Ilsebeth, wouldn't it?" Though too young for marriage, he already had a sweetheart in Swifthaven: Marco's younger sister, in fact.

"I'm sure she'll accept the news with her usual aplomb."

"She'll skin me alive and wear it as a trophy." Bert punctuated this macabre image with a chuckle, as though looking forward to the event. "Oh, stop glowering. The possibility that Leonie chooses either of us is nonexistent, especially if she avoids the party. Every eligible nobleman in the Twelve Kingdoms must be here tonight."

Indeed, men by far outnumbered women in the broad, lavish room. Married women outnumbered single ones, too, escoffions far more prevalent than exposed hair. The Princess of Elisia seemed to have no interest in competing for her suitors' attention.

A profusion of foods and flowers lined buttressed alcoves beneath high windows that showed the starry night sky. The room buzzed, its timbre low in the predominantly male crowd. Feminine laughter tinkled upon the air, like birdsong above a forest of cicadas. Marco found the brothers first, having trailed behind the Haukien diplomats that followed their new king. Shortly afterward, the trio happened upon Alois, who brimmed with pride at having greeted the princess at lunchtime.

"Did she laugh at you again?" Marco asked.

Alois brushed aside the question. "She laughs at everyone."

Several dignitaries intercepted Thorben, clasping his hands, extending salutations or condolences as their circumstances required. He had not expected his father's death to play such a significant part in this evening, but phantom memories accompanied him, of that visit long ago when the former King of Hauke had guided him much like he guided his younger brother now.

Perhaps he should have chosen to hunt in lands closer to home. Elisia had the best variety of game, but he might have killed a boar or a stag near Swifthaven and never brushed against these sobering feelings.

"Have we paid our half-hour yet?" he asked as melancholy set into his bones.

Bert grinned. Marco opened his mouth for a rebuke, but before a single word emerged, silence rippled across the room. As though enthralled, every head turned to the entrance and the ethereal figure that stood beneath its pointed arch.

Princess Leonie of Elisia shone like the light of a full moon, silvery-bright with the glitter of stars around her. Her pale hair, coiled and braided long, reflected the glow of the chandeliers. For one breathtaking moment, she surveyed her audience, a creature of grace and aristocratic poise.

Then her eyes crinkled and she laughed. "My, there are so many of you here! I swear I've sent at least half of you away before tonight!"

Chuckles echoed her mirth, for not a bite of malice tinged her pretty voice. She pitched it to the back of the company as she homed in on a portly gentleman nearby. "You there, the wine barrel. Haven't I told you I don't want your vineyards?"

The man's cheeks burned crimson as he smiled and nodded. She swept past him without another glance, a sylph in white gauze dancing in their midst.

"Tor," breathed Bert, rigid beside his older brother, "she's . . . she's . . ."

"Enchanting," Alois finished on a lovestruck sigh. He sprang from their group, intent upon intercepting the object of his devotion.

Thorben, jarring from his initial stupor, frowned. Leonie had certainly grown into a dazzling beauty, but her high spirits did her no credit. "She's insulting her guests."

Indeed, the princess had paused beside an elderly man, her chin tucked in laughing reproof. "Your Grace, you know that Death will embrace you before I do. He might be waiting on your doorstep even now." The company around the aged nobleman tittered, and he affected amusement that did not reflect in his eyes. Leonie had already moved on, careless of the havoc she wreaked.

Some swains she ignored, as though they didn't exist. Others she pretended not to know. When Alois stepped into her path, she paused, the corners of her mouth faintly curving upward in a charming ghost of a smile. "And you are . . . ?"

"Don't tease me so," he pled.

She laughed. "Ah, yes. The dullard. I don't want to live in Arbenia, and I don't want you here. When will that thick skull of yours allow the message to pass?"

"You are ravishing tonight, Leonie," he said, as though she hadn't spoken such unkind words.

Something akin to frustration chased across her face, with a peal of laughter in its wake.

Thorben, mortified for his friend, exchanged a telling glance with Marco beside him. Then, he did a double take. "Where's Bert?"

At some point during the spectacle, his brother had slipped away. Thorben spun, seeking a glimpse of the younger royal in the crowd. Marco snatched at his sleeve and pointed.

Bert had arrived in Leonie's path at roughly the same time as her father. King Eustis wore an expression of long-suffering as he greeted his daughter. She kissed the air beside his cheeks and said, "Well, Sire? I have presented myself as commanded."

"And I'm sure you'll find many handsome and eligible men eager to make your acquaintance," the king replied. Before she could respond, he whirled, catching sight of Bert. "And here's one, Prince Berthold of Hauke."

Thorben tensed, stopped from advancing only by Marco's iron grip on his sleeve. Leonie measured his brother in a glance, amusement bubbling from her lips.

"The merest beansprout! What are you doing here, you pup? You can barely be out of leading strings."

As the nearest company laughed—some from courtesy and others from malice—Bert joined with them.

"I don't want to marry you, Highness," he said, smiling. "I only wanted to look at perfection up close."

Her eyes flashed. "Then look quick, and run home before your nursemaid misses you."

Bert, far from taking offense, clasped the delicate hand she proffered him, all smiles as he shamelessly gazed at her.

"Ilsebeth will love this story," Marco said.

Thorben released the breath he had held, thankful that his brother at least maintained a particle of wit. "Do you think she's bewitched?"

His advisor shook his head. "No. Some like Alois are stupidly lovesick. She's making enemies of others, though."

Indeed, in her wake the portly vineyard owner and the aged earl both wore flat expressions, satisfied when she insulted others but otherwise sour.

"Leonie—" her father began, but she had already moved to her next victim.

"They forgot to dry you on the line after they got you wet," she chirped to a viscount with deep wrinkles etched into his face. When a debonair young man swept into a bow, her merriment boiled over. "I've told you to save your ridiculous acting for the stage, Rouven. I never carry suitable vegetables to throw."

"Leonie," King Eustis said again, more forcefully. She blinked, the picture of innocence peering up at him. After a controlled exhale, he motioned her deeper into the crowd. "I have guests I should like to introduce you to. I've told them of your *charm* and *good breeding.*"

A chuckle rumbled in her throat. "Why should they care about any such thing?"

He ignored the pert question, leading her first to an Elisian duke roughly his age, then to a baronet. Thorben, fascinated as she ridiculed each man in turn, realized too late that the king's chosen route circled to him.

"And of course," King Eustis was saying as he oriented his daughter toward the visiting monarch, "you remember King Thorben of Hauke from when you first met so many years ago."

Leonie froze, the merest hint of gaiety upon her lips. Her eyes—as blue as the far-off ocean in the north—connected with his. Had he been less cynical, less haunted in these halls, he might have drowned in that limpid gaze. Instead, he steeled himself against the mockery yet to come.

True to her reputation, Leonie delivered. "You have a dimple in your chin, like a bird nipped you with its sharp beak. They should call you King Thrushbeard instead."

Then she laughed and turned away, once again confirming that she held him beneath her contempt. Laughter rang in his ears, fellow guests jostling him, clapping his shoulders, commenting what a good sport "King Thrushbeard" was. He had barely time to process, for that insult seemed the last that King Eustis would allow.

"*Leonie*," the monarch roared, and the whole room deadened. Slowly the princess turned, self-possessed as she regarded her seething father. The trembling in his hands carried to his voice. "I have provided you with everything you could ever possibly want. I *command* you to choose a husband."

The whole room seemed carved in stone, all eyes trained upon the pair of Elisian royals.

Princess Leonie blinked, slowly, and said, "No."

A gasp whispered through the crowd. Even Thorben, disconnected though he felt, gaped at her blatant refusal.

"You won't choose?" her father asked in deathly tones.

She shrugged, as though declining the offer of a new bauble. "I don't want anyone here."

"Then I will choose for you."

Her mirth vanished at last. "You cannot, sir."

On a growl, he stalked forward, snatching her arm before she could retreat. Fear flashed through her ocean eyes as he thrust his face close. "I will marry you to the first beggar who presents himself at my door."

She stared at him, almost nose to nose, her breath short in her lungs. Thorben strained to hear her incredulous response.

"You wouldn't."

"I will."

Another tense moment passed and then—

She laughed, wrenching out of his hold. "What a fine father you are! Surely no lady in the Twelve Kingdoms has ever been so blessed as I am!" Rather than give him opportunity to respond, she spun, striding for the exit and waving sunnily as she left. "Bow before your beggar princess, everyone. I must prepare for my imminent swain!"

Near the door, the Duke of Ursinbau intercepted her. She paused long enough to listen to his low words, but she only smiled and shrugged in response. A cloud of hostility left the room on her heels, as did the duke.

"Poor beggar," Marco said. "If not even her father can handle her, she'll run roughshod over a peasant."

Thorben, annoyed, searched the muttering crowd for his brother. "Our half-hour is definitely gone. Whatever her fate, it has nothing to do with me."

CHAPTER 3

Departing the castle proved easy, but escaping the effects of its disastrous party, not so much. Whispers of "King Thrushbeard" followed Thorben all the way to the exit and into the night.

"We shouldn't have left so quickly," Marco said, keeping pace with the pair of royals and their diplomatic guard. "You're only going to fuel the rumors."

"What rumors?" the young king asked, scowling.

"That you were the favored suitor tonight."

He stopped short and stared. "What?"

Marco propped his hands on his hips, like a tutor scolding his student. "King Eustis wanted his daughter to choose you. Everyone was speculating it from the moment you arrived. That he led her directly to you only reinforced the rumor. And now, you stalking away after her insult will confirm it."

"There's nothing between us, and there never was," Thorben snapped.

"Truth and rumor can walk the same paths. Everyone in there was watching you, gauging your interest, checking your reactions. They'll draw the easiest conclusion." Grudgingly he added, "It didn't help that you were awestruck in front of her."

"I wasn't—!"

"You didn't say a word."

"No one would blame you," Bert spoke up before the king could defend himself. "Or, they shouldn't. I've never seen a creature so exquisite."

Thorben shot him a narrow-eyed glare. "How would Ilsebeth feel if she heard you?"

"We'll find out when I tell her," the prince replied. "She'll want to hear every last detail, and probably want to see Leonie for herself."

A glance toward Marco showed no concern in that corner either. The advisor shrugged. "Ilsebeth knows she has him on a string. He's not straying, so she has no reason for jealousy."

That emotion flitted briefly through Thorben, though, that his younger brother could have such a confident relationship already. As king, he was destined to spend the rest of his life assuming whomever he married did so for a crown rather than affection towards the man who wore it.

Bert clapped him on the back, misreading the cause of his introspection. "Cheer up, Thrushbeard. At least they're not pronouncing your name wrong anymore." He chuckled and started down the street again. Thorben shifted his scowl to Marco, who merely shrugged.

"It's a silly title. It'll die before the sun rises tomorrow."

This prophecy did not prove true. That night, diplomats returning from the castle told the story to those who had remained at the embassy, some with quiet indignation and others with joviality. By morning, every servant and guard had heard the tale. Gereon hesitantly addressed it when he arrived to help his king dress.

Thorben, brooding, sent him away before his morning shave.

Alois arrived near noon, greeting the king at breakfast with, "Hallo, Thrushbeard, old fellow!" He clapped Thorben on the back, self-satisfaction permeating him. "Bit scruffy today, are we? Well, I'm sure that no one at the lodge will mind."

"Shouldn't you be playing the role of beggar on the king's doorstep?" Thorben asked. "Or has someone else already claimed your ill-mannered princess?"

"Psh." The Prince of Arbenia waved aside these worries with limp fingers. "King Eustis won't follow through with such an undignified threat. Marry Leonie to a beggar? The idea boggles the mind. Besides," he added, plucking up an apple from a basket on the table, "there aren't any beggars left in Felstark to claim her."

"What?" Marco, sitting across from his king, paused with knife halfway through a sausage. He leveled an incredulous look upon the newcomer.

"It's true," Alois said. "Ursinbau had them all rounded up and taken beyond the city walls last night, as soon as the king made his declaration. It's anyone's guess what happened to them from there, but the duke has command of the military, so it's his right."

"Then he at least took the threat seriously," said Marco.

Alois, biting into his apple, shook his head. He chewed and half-swallowed, spitting juice as he replied, "Give it a few days and King Eustis will retract his promise. He can't marry a jewel to a particle of dust."

"It would serve her right if he did," Thorben grumbled, unaccountably annoyed at the duke's efficiency.

Alois ignored this remark. "How soon are we going? I invited some of the gents from last night, and a few have already set out, so we shouldn't linger too long." When blank stares met this disclosure, he elaborated. "The castle wants people gone. It seemed the right thing to do. It's only Eligor, Jander, and Ivo and—oh! You know Florian of Vasberg and his brother, what's-his-name. They're all looking forward to a week of sport with the infamous Thrushbeard himself."

Thorben blinked, certain he was imagining this nonsense.

Marco, with more self-possession, beaned Alois in the head with a fresh-baked croissant. "You blunderer! Why would you invite extras?"

"What's wrong with it?"

"Hauke doesn't have treaties with Vasberg, for one thing! That turns it from a retreat to a diplomatic meeting." He slammed his fork on the table, rising from his chair.

Alois raised defensive hands, wary of another pastry-based attack. "It's just schoolfellows."

"Not when one of us is a king now! Were they staying with you at the castle? Can we intercept them and send them home instead?"

"I told you they already left. They might be halfway to the lodge already, with my voucher to gain entrance."

Marco swore, then swiveled to his ruler. "Tor, I'm sorry. What do we do?"

"We can't go," Thorben said, disappointment sitting like an egg in his throat. "Or, more specifically, I can't. Nothing's stopping the rest of you—even Bert, if he wants."

His advisor scoffed. "And what, leave you to wend your way home alone?"

"Or cool my heels here until you pass this way again."

Alois rocked from one foot to the other. "You're both making too much of this. It's only a hunting trip. The more the merrier, I say."

Marco swatted at him over the table, missing by several inches. "Then have fun joining them. We're going back to Hauke."

"Are we?" Thorben's quiet words cut through the tension in the dining room, arresting the pair of bickering men. He lifted somber eyes to his advisor. "I was supposed to be gone for two weeks. If I come back early, after attending only a party in Felstark, won't that create more of your rumors?"

"Who cares about rumors, Tor?" Marco said.

"You did, last night."

A heavy breath pushed out of Marco's nose. He made no attempt to recant his concerns for his king's reputation. Reluctantly Thorben sighed. "I should break the news to Bert."

"You can't be serious," said Alois, like a child three seconds from a tantrum.

Marco flung a finger toward the doorway. "You get out of here. Go find your princess her stag's antlers."

The Prince of Arbenia hesitated, as though expecting them both to burst into laughter and declare their behavior a capital joke. When no such declaration came, he shook his head. "So touchy about a silly little name," he muttered, and he slammed the door behind him when he left.

"Dullard," said Marco to the wood panels.

Thorben, loath to give Leonie any credit for perception, silently agreed that her insult of Alois had been apt.

Perhaps her insult of him was apt as well.

"Are you really not going to shave?" Bert asked two days later.

Thorben, stretched out on a velvet couch in the embassy's diplomatic quarters, tossed a brass paperweight in the shape of a fish, up and down, up and down. Thick brown bristles covered his jaw, much to his valet's increasing horror. "Why should I? If everyone's calling me Thrushbeard, I might as well look the part."

Of course people weren't calling him that to his face. They only talked about it behind his back. The women in the embassy thought the nickname cute and the men found it amusing. When he'd taken refuge in the garden the previous afternoon, he'd even overheard children discussing it beyond the wall: "That building belongs to Hauke, where King Thrushbeard reigns."

The simple insult had traveled from the castle into the city itself, which gave him little hope it would end there. Every time he heard it whispered, his heart calcified a fraction more against Princess Leonie.

She deserved to marry a beggar, to tumble from her lofty tower and dwell in the mud. Perhaps she could gain a shred of compassion then instead of offending everyone she met.

But that would never happen. The Duke of Ursinbau proved a better steward than her father, his soldiers patrolling the streets that surrounded Felstark Castle day and night. No beggar could get within a hundred yards of the entrance. Time would calm King Eustis's fury, and Leonie would face no real consequences for her treatment of Thorben or anyone else.

"Shall I grow one as well?" Bert asked, rubbing his smooth chin with a speculative gleam in his eyes.

"Can you?" Thorben wryly asked. Gereon would have a fit if both of them refused his morning attentions, but Bert was too young to shave every day anyway. Any beard he tried to grow would come in patchy at best.

The younger brother swatted the elder's feet and plopped down on the cushion where they rested. Thorben tented his legs, spared Bert a dry glance, and tossed the brass fish up and down again.

"You need to get out," Bert said. "You're never fun when you're brooding."

"Where am I supposed to go? On the streets for people to mock me there? I'm not even officially crowned yet, but I'm certainly branded."

"It was a silly insult. It only has legs because the one who spoke it is the most beautiful creature in the world."

"You're not helping," said Thorben wryly.

His brother shrugged. "I kind of feel sorry for her. Every story out of the castle makes it seem like she really did take a vow of celibacy. She hates marriage, that much is certain."

A scoff escaped the cynical young king. "What woman hates marriage?"

"I don't know. They say she discharges any maid or lady-in-waiting who weds, though."

Up and down went the paperweight, swimming through air instead of water. "If she wants to stay single, she should retire to a convent and spare the rest of us her questionable wit."

"Apparently she has a deathly fear of nuns."

Thorben caught the weight, its corners digging into his palms as he stared at his brother.

Bert chuckled. "I doubt that one's true, but I thought it was funny enough to pass along. If she has a deathly fear of anything, though, it should be beggars."

"She knows her father won't follow through," Thorben darkly said. "What king could marry his own daughter off like that?" He sat up, twisting to rest his feet upon the floor. The fish, clasped within his interlaced fingers, stared sightlessly up at him. Its huge eyes and rounded mouth conveyed shock, as though his handling had startled it.

"Wouldn't it be funny if a beggar came along and refused *her*?" Bert said, grinning.

"It would be poetic," said Thorben with a rueful laugh, "but things would never advance that far. I'm telling you, if any beggar gets past Ursinbau, King Eustis will dismiss his claim. He's probably changed his mind already."

They sat in silence for a long while, the ray of sunlight from the window stretching until it touched the young king's boots.

"You'd make a good beggar, what with how scraggly you look," said Bert.

Thorben shot him a sidelong glance of reproof. It failed to dampen the younger brother's amusement.

Instead, Bert's grin broadened. "We should give her a scare."

"Go play somewhere else, and take your silly ideas with you," Thorben said.

"No, but really." Caught in his flight of fancy, Bert sprang from the couch and began to pace. "We could dress up as a troupe of . . . of starving musicians, or something, and sneak past the guards to beg coins for our songs."

"Who is this 'we' in your disastrous plan? You think Marco will have any part of such idiocy?"

"Not Marco. He can't carry a tune in a bucket. But you and I both play the pipes, and Gereon can strike a tambourine."

"Oh, my valet is taking part? And how do you propose gaining his cooperation?"

"We'll promise him he can shave you once the trick is over."

Thorben swiped at his brother, who skirted out of the way, eyes dancing.

"It'll be fun, Tor, just the thing to lighten your mood."

"Take your ridiculous schemes somewhere else. We're not playing beggars and that's that."

Bert left as commanded, but when a pair of shepherd's pipes appeared at the supper table, it was apparent he hadn't abandoned his proposed prank. Thorben had learned the instrument as a child—all the princes and princesses of Hauke had, as a sort of protest when their mother insisted they have music lessons. They'd all chosen the easiest, most obnoxious option they could find in hopes that Queen Julika would change her mind.

She didn't, and now had four children who could pipe with varying degrees of success.

Thorben had no intention of begging even as a joke, but he toyed with one of the pipes that night in his room. The Elisian castle loomed in full view from his balcony, lights bright in its windows as though its occupants harbored not a care in the world.

It might be fun to play Bert's childish prank, but the royals would certainly recognize him. Doubtless such a discovery would add to whatever rumors still flew, the King of Hauke trying to win a bride by subterfuge after she rejected him to his face.

"The beard has to go," said Marco the following morning. "You hardly look like yourself anymore."

Across the breakfast table, Bert waggled his eyebrows at his brother.

Thorben ignored him. "We're supposed to be hunting. Why shouldn't I return home looking like a woodsman?"

Marco, oblivious to the siblings' silent interaction, raked his knife through his eggs and speared a runny segment. "Because you brought your very fastidious valet along, and his pride would be wounded for others to see you like this."

"At least with a beard no one has to look at my unsightly chin."

Marco banked his bite of egg in one cheek and stared at his king. "You have a very nice chin. Most women love dimples."

"Did you conduct a poll?" Thorben blandly asked. "You should've asked their opinions on nuns as well."

Bert snorted into his cup of tea.

Marco, with no context for this remark, glanced between the pair suspiciously. "Why do you care what she said, Tor? Have you been in love with her all along?"

"Only if love is a bilious feeling." He cast his napkin aside and slouched in his chair. "It's not the insult itself, but how far it's run and the knowledge that she'll face no consequences for it. I can't insult her back. That would be beneath me as both a gentleman and a king. So instead, I have to sit with dignity as others mock me behind my back—and some of them to my face. You think Alois is the only one who's going to use that name for me?"

"So you want revenge," Marco surmised. "Shall we declare war?" When Thorben bucked his head, the advisor lifted upturned palms. "Is that not enough? Too much? What would satisfy you?"

"An apology."

"We both know you're not getting one of those."

That rankled like a bur beneath his clothes, next to his skin. "I know," he muttered, and he pushed away from the table.

He spent the morning in the garden, playing on his borrowed pipe. When a second answered in countermelody, he glanced up to discover Bert on the balcony above, mischief tugging at his pursed lips.

They weren't professionals by any stretch of the imagination, but they could create a tune jaunty enough to raise Thorben's spirits. He returned to his quarters in a much better mood.

Once, there, he discovered Bert's next present: a set of ragged clothes, procured from who-knew-where, with a vague smell of earth and campfire clinging to the dingy fabric.

CHAPTER 4

We're not going to the castle," said Thorben, twiddling the pipe he carried. A late afternoon breeze wove around him, finding every threadbare patch of the ragged clothes he wore.

"No, of course not," said Bert, who glanced to the third member of their party as though expecting confirmation.

Gereon, somehow looking stiff and starched despite his shabby suit, arched a critical brow. He said nothing, but the tambourine he carried jingled with every step. The skies alone knew where Bert had scrounged up that instrument in addition to the pipes, to say nothing of their worn clothing. Thorben trilled a few notes on his pipe, drawing attention from a handful of nearby pedestrians.

They looked away just as quickly, clueless that the King of Hauke strode in their midst. After four days cooped up in his country's embassy, hypersensitive to every glance in his direction, it felt good to get out, to walk, to blend in with a crowd.

"If we did happen on the castle," Bert said jovially, "you could openly refuse to marry the princess."

Thorben hummed, playing along. "She could marry you instead."

"I'd cry off on Ilsebeth's account, and Gereon's married already and too old by far. So," the prince concluded with a shrug, "none of us is available. She'll have to suffer a jilt."

As entertaining as this imagined scenario was, they were walking the opposite direction, toward the marketplace near the west gate to try their hand at busking.

"We're far more likely to get arrested and thrown from the city," Thorben said, almost hoping for this potential outcome. Most of the visiting nobles had left Felstark already, and people assumed the King of Hauke had gone with them. He was, after all, meant to stay only one night.

Now, days later, he risked drawing undue attention when he officially vacated his embassy. People might speculate that he'd remained to plead his suit with the Elisian princess, and Thorben was loath for anyone to draw a connection between him and her.

Thus, if the Duke of Ursinbau mistook him for a beggar and cast him from the city walls, he could vanish without any pomp or false assumptions. Marco could escort the horses and luggage from the city and join them on the road, and they could return to Swifthaven at their leisure.

Presuming the advisor didn't march them straight home. Thorben had only left him a note, and Bert had left behind no word at all.

"He'll ruin our fun if he gets half a chance," the young prince had said.

Marco certainly would. Even Gereon would've threatened the excursion were it not for Thorben's promised appointment with a razor blade once the ruse ended.

Thorben had prowled the streets of Swifthaven often in his youth, back before his father's death. Felstark was similar enough to invoke that nostalgia. Plump gray clouds foretold a summer shower, the smell of rain thick upon the air. He piped a tune as they walked, and Bert soon added harmony. Each note seemed to buoy him, until he bounced from one step to another, careless of any attention he drew in his tattered clothes.

Gereon strode beside them, rolling his eyes as he half-heartedly beat the tambourine against his leg. Their felt hats, too floppy in the brims, kept the cloud-filtered sunlight off their faces and spits of rain off their heads.

The market, subdued on such a gray afternoon, provided plenty of venues for their impromptu concert. They parked on a corner and played, careless of the copper coins tossed at their feet. Tor and Bert mostly knew Haukien folksongs, and they took turns playing melodies and countermelodies, botching one or the other often enough to break off the song in laughter. Gereon, as percussion, remained stone-faced, an anchor of dignity to the brothers' mirth.

Soldiers and city guards eyed them in passing but never stopped. One took up post on the opposite corner, arms folded as he watched the trio, but he never approached.

"Maybe he's waiting for us to finish," Thorben said between songs, his heartbeat erratic in his chest.

"He's waiting for us to pick up the coins," Bert replied, wiping his pipe's mouthpiece on his ragged shirt hem. "There's no law against playing music in the street, but the minute we accept money for it, we fall under the duke's temporary ban on begging."

Thorben's brows arched. "Where did you learn that?"

His brother grinned. "I asked around. Shall we get ourselves cast from the city?"

Tempting as this prospect was, the impending storm would make such a removal uncomfortable. Thorben pressed his pipe to his lips and started another tune. The coin offerings shifted from copper to silver. When someone tossed a gold piece, he realized the citizens of Felstark were baiting them, hoping they would get themselves ejected.

At least they would have funds enough to spend the night somewhere down the road, if they chose that fate.

When thunder started rolling across the darkening sky, Thorben tucked his pipe into his belt and flexed his stiffened fingers. Stalls and shops were closing, people hurrying home before the full brunt of the storm could drench them. Bert, shrugging, tucked away his pipe as well, and they started back up the road, leaving a collection of glittering coins for their audience of one. The soldier, at first surprised that they would abandon such bounty, darted across the road to gather it before they'd gone even halfway up the street.

A flash of lightning and a deafening crack signaled the clouds to open. Rain dumped on them, falling in sheets against a sudden gust of wind.

"Run!" Thorben cried, holding his tattered hat to his head. They dashed from one awning to the next as darkness filled the streets.

Somewhere along the way, they took a wrong turn, evident when Gereon, in the lead, paused and pivoted a full circle. Thorben dragged him to a covered porch where Bert, teeth chattering, had already taken refuge.

"How far are we from the embassy, do you think?" the young king asked.

His valet shook his head, pointing first one direction and then the opposite way. An upward glance gave them no clues. The clouds had lowered, obscuring the castle towers from sight, destroying any hope of using that landmark to orient themselves.

"Marco's going to kill us," Thorben muttered.

"I think it's that way," said Bert, pointing the first direction the valet had. "I remember passing that blue door."

Already soaked, they had no reason not to continue. Rain fell like needles as they bolted from one doorway to the next. The storm engulfed the mountain city, mist obscuring their view.

Far from fearful, Thorben wanted to laugh. Although the downpour was cool it was not frigid, and he rather enjoyed its wildness after days of moping. They paused beneath a wide, pointed arch to check their bearings—a useless attempt once again. His breath puffed into the descending night.

They were in the highest ward of Felstark, certainly, but they seemed to be going in circles. Gereon, scowling, silently counted on his fingers, lips moving as he retraced the turns they should have taken. Bert, meanwhile, peered into the soupy night and said, "We might have to wait this out, Tor. I don't recognize anything here."

Before Thorben could answer, the door behind them opened, bathing them in a warm, orange glow and a rich, savory aroma. As they turned, a kitchen maid halted on the threshold, a tub of dirty dishwater perched on her hip. She regarded them with huge eyes. The white of her small cap revealed dark hair in tidy braids, her charcoal-colored uniform and snowy apron emblems of a noble household.

"Sorry," said Thorben, stepping aside to let her throw her water to the street. "We only paused here for a moment's shelter."

She didn't move. Behind her, the other occupants of the kitchen stilled, the clink of dishes dying against the steady downpour. When a gust of wind sprayed inward across the girl's face, she flinched and looked back over her shoulder. Within the room, a broad-shouldered cook hastily wiped his hands and cast his towel aside.

"Come in," he said, beckoning. Someone behind him hissed, but he ignored it. "We can't leave people out in such a storm."

Thorben hung back, reluctant to enter the unknown residence, but Bert bounded past the dish maid and headed straight for the huge, bright-burning hearth. "Thank you! We got caught out on our way back to our lodgings, and the mist has turned us around." He extended his hands toward the flames, rubbing them.

Thorben exchanged a glance with Gereon. The valet motioned him into the kitchen, refusing to enter before his master did. The door shut behind them, cutting off the blustering storm; the dish maid returned her tub to the counter, dirty suds still sloshing within it.

A dozen servants occupied the broad kitchen, and not one of them moved as Thorben and Gereon joined Bert at the fire.

"Whereabouts are you staying?" the head cook asked, an odd tension in his voice.

Thorben shot a warning glance toward his brother and answered vaguely. "It's somewhere in this area. We're not from Felstark, but our hosts were kind enough to lend us space until we move on."

"We're musicians," Bert chirped. "We spent all afternoon playing in the market."

If anything, this added to the tension in the room. The cook licked his lips, sweat beading on his forehead. "Did you earn a lot?"

"Oh, we had *so* many coins tossed at us! It was a jolly time!"

Thorben elbowed his brother and minutely shook his head. True, they had played beggars all afternoon, but the noble households were more likely to follow Ursinbau's decree. Getting tossed from the city walls this late and in this weather would spell disaster.

Behind the cook, though, a kitchen boy slipped through a doorway and vanished down a shadowed corridor.

"We don't need to stay," Thorben said. "If you can just direct us to—"

"Of course you'll stay," the cook interrupted. "We can't turn away anyone on our doorstep, especially not in a storm like this.

Have you eaten? We have stew almost ready. Would you care to trade a song for a meal?"

Apprehension filled the young king's throat. Was this entrapment, like the soldier across the street waiting for them to collect their earnings? "Maybe we can play once our joints thaw, if the storm doesn't let up. Our hosts will be worried if we don't return soon, though."

By now Marco would have discovered his scribbled excuses. Likely he was ordering all of Hauke's diplomats to scour the city.

How far was the embassy from here? They should have started back half an hour earlier, before the storm could descend in full. The cook, for the moment satisfied with a delay in any beggarly transactions, turned his attention to chopping onions on a huge butcher block. As if following this cue, the rest of the servants resumed their tasks, though they often stole glances at the trio by the fire.

Thorben removed his drooping hat and wrung the water from his patched cloak, conscious of the bedraggled picture he posed. His gaze traveled the walls around him, seeking a crest or coat of arms to signify whose house they had invaded. A leaden feeling settled in his gut.

There were no emblems, no markings on the stacks of plain ceramic dishes, no seals on the earthen cups. The dinnerware here wouldn't grace a noble table.

Meaning this kitchen was for the household servants. An extra kitchen, a luxury that only the most prestigious nobles would have—or the castle itself.

"Where are we?" Thorben started to ask, but swift, heavy footsteps echoed along the darkened corridor. Although bracing for the worst, he still cringed when King Eustis of Elisia latched onto the door frame.

CHAPTER 5

Yes. *At last.*" Satisfaction descended on the King of Elisia's face, and low, exultant triumph infused his voice. As he surveyed the sodden trio, no spark of recognition flashed into his eyes. Even so, Thorben instinctively shifted to block Bert—the most easily identifiable—from sight.

How could they be so stupid as to pause on the castle's very doorstep? They must have circled around to a back aspect, where the lowest of the royal kitchens allowed access to the city itself. And Ursinbau's posted soldiers must have taken refuge indoors, presuming no beggars foolish enough to brave such a downpour.

King Eustis pinned a stern stare upon the head cook. "Keep them here," he said and swept back down the hall as quickly as he had appeared.

"Yes," Bert hissed, eyes alight with glee in the Elisian king's retreat. Thorben shot him an incredulous glance, but the prince merely leaned a fraction closer. "You can have your revenge, Tor. The beggar can reject the princess."

"And if they realize who we are, we've caused an international conflict," Thorben whispered back. Their best option was to play dumb. He pivoted, uneasy with how many servants now stood between him and the exit. He singled out the head cook among them. "Have we done something to offend?"

"No," said that man in a hollow voice. "I believe the king intends to honor you. Or, one of you."

"A moment by the fire was honor enough. We shouldn't trouble you further."

"We had orders to allow entrance to any beggars on our doorstep, and now we have orders to keep you here."

Thorben's heartbeat raced. "But we're not beggars. We're musicians." A glance around the room showed that their audience saw no distinction between the two categories. He swallowed, continuing his charade of ignorance. "What sort of honor?"

"The king himself will tell you, if he wishes to bestow it. Perhaps he'll change his mind."

Or perhaps Ursinbau would arrive first and strong-arm them from the castle. Did the duke live here or elsewhere? Thorben felt certain he could smooth over the mistake with the Elisian heir if they were out and away from the king.

His brother poked him in the ribs and hissed, "Relax. No one looks for royalty in rags. We can decline the king's offer and be on our way into the night."

"This is your fault," Thorben hissed back.

"And it's a grand lark. He can't force anyone to marry."

True as this seemed, the gleam in King Eustis's eyes implied otherwise.

But then, maybe he merely wanted to scare his daughter into better behavior. He might show her the trio of beggars, demand she choose from them, and then concede to give her another chance among her peers. The power struggle between father and daughter obviously burned bright, and what better way to assert his superiority?

But Leonie—willful, laughing, unpredictable Leonie—might complicate matters.

Too soon, footsteps echoed in the passage again. Castle guards entered the kitchen, scowling at the three by the fire. Their armor clinked as they took posts by each exit.

If Thorben declared himself now, he could start a war. The Elisians were detaining a foreign monarch by force.

And his mother would burst a vein when she learned of this evening, especially if it brought them into conflict with an allied kingdom.

When a dazed-looking priest joined the kitchen crowd, though, war seemed suddenly appealing. How far would King Eustis push his ridiculous threat? Thorben ran a hand along his chin, taking comfort in the bristles that hid his telltale dimple. If he could skate out of this crisis unrecognized, the beard would have served him well.

His tattered clothing had gone from soaked to merely damp by the time King Eustis dragged a haughty Leonie into the kitchen. She was no less beautiful for a lack of ornaments.

Instead, her plain white dress complimented her as admirably as the evening gown of a few nights ago. A lady's maid with blazing red hair trailed fretfully behind them, wringing the end of her long braid.

The princess tipped her chin into the air. Her blue eyes flitted across the too-crowded space, her mouth quirked as though mockery sat upon her tongue. "Well, sir?" she said to her father.

He pointed toward the hearth. "Your groom stands by the fire. I needed only one, and Providence sent us three. Perhaps you may choose after all."

"A pair of derelicts and a bantling? I'm not choosing any of them. I've already told you I don't want to marry."

"And I've already sworn that you will. The choice is mine, then."

He dropped his hold upon her. She looked like she might bolt, but two guards already blocked the hallway from which she had emerged. So, instead, she folded her arms, making ready to challenge whatever her father declared.

King Eustis descended on the sodden trio. Bert, still convinced this was a fine bit of sport, bounced on his heels. Gereon shrank back as though trying to blend in with the warm bricks that lined the hearth. Thorben, with increasing frustration, bowed his head in a sign of obeisance, eyes fixed on the king's feet. The man was wearing scarlet house slippers, the toes nonsensically curled.

"One of you shall marry my daughter this evening." King Eustis touched Thorben's chin to lift his gaze, the better to assess him. Thorben avoided eye contact, his attention flitting past his shoulder to Leonie and her maid.

The princess did not recognize him from afar, and neither did her father up close.

"You'll do," said the king, dropping his hand.

"Oh, no, sire," said Thorben.

King Eustis paused mid-turn, arching his brow, a deathly stare upon his face.

Thorben swallowed. "There's a mistake. We were only caught in the storm and came here by accident."

"Beggars on my doorstep will accept what they are given. I'm giving you my daughter."

"I don't want her."

A stricken hush fell across the room. Leonie, spine straight, stared directly at him. The wideness of her eyes held not dismay, nor insult, but a strange and half-wild *hope*.

"You will accept her hand or be horsewhipped," said King Eustis.

A short, rueful sigh escaped Thorben's lips. There was nothing for it but to announce himself, to reveal the mortifying charade and face whatever consequences befell him and Hauke both. Before a single word could leave his tongue, though, Leonie spoke.

"Horsewhip him, then, for I shan't have him."

"You're the one who should be horsewhipped," he snapped. Her brows rose, but her flippant air didn't diminish one whit.

King Eustis growled. "You'll both be horsewhipped, then married by proxy while you heal. I have decreed a wedding and it shall take place before a single soul leaves this room."

"What if he's already married?" Leonie asked.

"Then he's about to commit bigamy. You can battle it out with the other wife when you meet her." He motioned to the priest. "Reverend Father, if you would kindly perform the rites."

The priest, far from objecting to this unorthodox arrangement, stepped into the broad space between the unwilling bride and groom. He pulled a small prayerbook from his voluminous sleeve and thumbed its pages.

"You can't—" Thorben started, his heartbeat escalating.

"Silence," Eustis said, "or I'll cut you down myself."

The threat, far from cowing the King of Hauke, ignited his fury. A black cloud descended on him. The man would force his daughter on an objecting party? It didn't matter if it was beggar or monarch-in-disguise; such treatment was wrong.

Bert tugged on his sleeve, cognizant at last that this prank had twisted far beyond its original intent. "Tor, we can't—"

King Eustis caught the quiet words. "Is that your name? Tor? As plain a name as she deserves alliance with. Leonie, stand beside your groom."

She tightened her folded arms, fists clenched. "I won't."

"Horsewhipped and sent to a convent, then?"

The blood drained from her face. To Thorben's shock, she flounced across the intervening space and spun, taking her decreed position in the farcical ceremony. Her maid, left behind, worried her lower lip. Not a servant or guard moved, all eyes riveted on the spectacle.

The priest intoned a marriage rite, never asking consent from either party. It was over almost as quickly as it began, ending with a solemn declaration that the mismatched pair was now husband and wife.

"Give them a bowl of soup for their wedding feast, then cast them out," King Eustis said. "Beggars don't belong under my roof."

As he strode callously from the kitchen, Leonie's maid surged past him to clasp her mistress's hands. Leonie stood like a statue, rigid, unseeing, and the girl babbled. "I'll come with you, miss. I'll send a message to my mum and dad—"

"You can't," the princess said, scorn in her voice. "What beggar has a maid? How am I to pay your wages?"

"I don't need—!"

"Go home, Gitta. You can marry your sweetheart with a clear conscience now, and never give me another thought."

"I won't! Your Highness—!"

"Can I beg some proper shoes, do you think? Or a cloak? I doubt my estimable husband can provide such articles." She slid a cagey glance toward Thorben and away again.

All too familiar with that sort of snub from her, he buttoned his lips. By some miracle, the royals of Elisia had not recognized their foreign peer. Perhaps it would do Leonie some good to think herself a beggar instead of telling her a king stood beside her.

The marriage itself couldn't be valid, not after such a slapdash ceremony. He might string her along for a few days, let her suffer, and then set her free to wander as she pleased. If he could determine for sure that the marriage was a sham, he might never even reveal his true identity.

He certainly wasn't taking her home to his mother. Nor was he shaving until she departed on her own path. The beggar charade would have to extend beyond an afternoon.

The cook ladled bowls of stew that no one stepped forward to receive. Savory broth steamed upon the air, and servants drifted toward the exit, allowed to pass the guards who remained in position. Leonie's maid, Gitta, vanished.

"Tor," Bert whispered, tugging at his brother's sleeve again, "what do we do?"

Thorben, still in the throes of cynicism, said, "We should probably eat. Beggars don't often get a hot meal." So saying, he plopped into one of the chairs at the counter and pulled a bowl of stew in front of him. The broth scalded his tongue, but he couldn't taste anything anyway. After three spoonfuls, he cast a glance over his shoulder toward where Leonie stood as though carved from marble. "You should eat too. Never know when the next meal might come."

She jerked as though summoned from a reverie. A scowl puckered her lovely brows, all evidence of her former mirth gone. With stilted gait she joined him at the counter, but she only played with the bowl she was given, spooning broth and letting it fall again.

Bert and Gereon warily joined them, following Thorben's example. Gitta shortly reappeared, arms laden with bundles of fabric and a pair of sturdy boots dangling by their ties from her elbow. She dumped the load on a stretch of countertop and concentrated on unknotting the bootlaces.

Leonie picked at a flimsy piece of white linen. "What is this?"

"I brought you a wimple, Your Highness."

She cast it away as though it were a snake. "You know I hate them. I won't wear it."

"Leonie, you *must*. A married woman has to cover her hair."

"No one will care if a beggar covers her hair or not."

The maid stopped her task to grasp her lady's shoulders. "People will very much care. You've never lived beyond the castle before. You won't have the same protection out there that you have here, and you have no idea what it's like for an unmarried woman. The wimple signals that someone is responsible for you, that you're not alone in the world."

"I *hate* them," Leonie hissed, nose-to-nose with the redhead.

"You hate when *other people* wear them," Gitta hissed back. She glanced beyond her mistress, briefly meeting Thorben's curious gaze and looking away again—distracted just long enough for Leonie to pinch her wrist. "Ouch! I'm sorry! All I'm saying is it shouldn't bother you to wear one yourself!" She snatched up the length of linen and draped it over the princess's head, arranging it to hide her golden hair.

All the while, Leonie glowered at her.

Gitta stepped back. "You look beautiful, as always."

If anything, the comment enraged her mistress even more. "If you like it so much, *you* wear it!" She tore the head covering off and flung it at her startled maid, then snatched up the boots to jam her feet into them one after the other. "Are the beggars done with their meal yet? I'm sure you heard the king: we don't belong under his precious roof."

"Your Highness—" the head cook began.

"I'm not 'Your Highness' anymore," she snapped. "I'm a nameless, faceless beggar's wife. Gitta, go home and marry your insipid lover. Wear your horrid wimple and blend in with the masses." She stood, stamping her feet to settle them in the sturdy shoes. Her maid stooped to tie the laces before the princess could.

"It's still raining," the cook faintly said.

Leonie snorted. "The first of many storms I'll have to weather, no doubt." She swiped up the darker length of fabric Gitta had brought, a long cloak, and swept it around her shoulders.

Meanwhile, Thorben languidly chewed his last bite of vegetables from the stew, in no mood to accommodate her haste.

The cook swiveled to him, half hope. "You said you had lodgings in the area . . . ?"

"Men only," he lied. "We'll have to see if one of the inns in the lower city wards have space in their common room." As royalty, he'd never spent the night in such a place, but he'd heard tales of such escapades from his noble peers, scions who had ventured out into the world on a lark or a dare. In fact, Alois had once spent a week in a rural hostelry in Nikelberg, a tale he'd recounted at least a dozen times.

Speaking of Alois, he would have Thorben's head if he ever learned of tonight's events. As blundering as the second Prince of Arbenia could be, he'd been a friend since childhood, and maintaining good relations with his kingdom was in Hauke's best interests. The young monarch tapped the countertop, adding this to the list of concerns he would have to attend.

The rhythmic drumming drew his new bride's attention. He paused, meeting her gaze, arching his brows in an unspoken prompt for her to speak her thoughts aloud.

Leonie made the same face at him, exaggerated to mock him.

He turned his back on her to address Bert and Gereon instead. "You'll have to go tell our hosts what happened. I'll send a message to let you know where the two of us end up for the night."

"So sorry to inconvenience you," Leonie said sarcastically.

He whirled, standing, a full head taller than her. "You *have* inconvenienced me, greatly. What fool would want such a wife?" Ignoring how she flinched, he snatched up his hat from the counter and rammed it on his head. As he strode to the exit, Bert and Gereon scrambled after him. He didn't bother to check whether Leonie followed.

The storm had calmed, but rain still fell in a steady whisper. He paused on the small porch long enough to raise the collar of his tattered coat. Then he started into the mist.

If they were at the castle, it was only a matter of following its walls until they recognized the road to their embassy.

"Tor," said Bert, jogging to catch up with him, tugging on his sleeve, "what are we doing?"

"*You* are going to confess your sins to Marco and start back with him to Hauke tomorrow. *I* am going to find the seediest inn in this city and hope that my blushing bride has *fleas* by dawn."

His brother stopped short, gaping. "You can't—!"

Thorben, pausing to arch a brow at him, looked back up the road. Leonie trailed them, the hood of her cloak shielding her golden hair from the rain. Gereon, ever the gentleman's valet, kept pace near her, ready to offer any assistance she might require.

A twinge of compunction touched Thorben's heart, but he brushed it aside. This wasn't a true marriage, and the princess didn't deserve his compassion in her fall from grace.

Bert sidled closer to him, lowering his voice as the pair approached. "Marco won't stand for you staying in an inn like a commoner. You'll be surrounded by Haukien guards before morning. Just tell her who you really are."

"Never in a *thousand years*," Thorben hissed, and he resumed his trek through the drizzle.

True to his expectations, the castle wall led them to more familiar surroundings. When the main gate appeared, haloed in yellow light from lanterns around it, he knew exactly where they were.

He stopped long enough for the others to catch up. "We part ways here. Bert, Gereon, you can find your way back." His valet opened his mouth, but a pointed glare and a shake of his head stopped the protest. This was an order, and the servant would obey without question.

Leonie, frowning as she observed, said nothing. She maintained her silence as Bert and Gereon departed. Thorben buried his hands in his pockets and took a road he knew would lead to the less affluent city wards.

A patter of footsteps, surprisingly light in boots so sturdy, followed him.

Porches extended over many of the walkways along their chosen route, allowing some shelter from the rain. Leonie trotted to join him before they'd gone a full block.

"What did you say your name was?" she asked. "I didn't hear it properly."

He indulged his petty streak. "I don't have one, remember? I'm just a nameless, faceless beggar."

"Well, I have to call you something. Should I give you a name, then?"

He flinched despite himself. "My friends call me Tor," he said before she could choose anything too ridiculous—like *Thrushbeard*.

"Is that a nickname?"

"Yes. It's short for 'dictator.'"

"Makes sense, what with how you order them around."

"Exactly."

With swiftness he had not expected, she swept in front of him and whirled to block his path. "Tor."

He stopped short, confused. The faint, diffused light around them gleamed in her eyes and highlighted the droplets that clung to her hood, to her hair, to her eyelashes.

"I didn't want to get married," Leonie said.

"Neither did I," he replied, childishly.

They stood in silence, then, each assessing the other. The longer he stared, the more lovely she looked, like a distant star in a cold night sky. He caged his heart against such treacherous thoughts. This was temporary, an arrangement he would discard as soon as he responsibly could.

Besides, Leonie was looking through him, not at him. "Do you always wear that ratty hat?" she suddenly asked.

Had she caught a hint of recognition at last? He reached for the hat, self-conscious.

She shrieked. "Don't take it off! I only asked if you always wore it!"

"You called it ratty," he said, bewildered and defensive as he tugged the sodden brim more firmly in place.

"That doesn't mean it can't be worn."

"Then why ask?"

"I was only trying to—" Her voice cut out in disgust. "Never mind." She spun and continued down the street. When Thorben hesitated to follow, she cast over her shoulder, "I don't know where I'm going, Tor."

Despite this confession, she kept her purposeful stride. He jogged the short distance and fell in step beside her. "You don't know your own city?"

A cynical grunt left her lips. "Why would I need to? I always had an escort before."

"Well, I don't know where I'm going either. I was only passing through Felstark."

"Going where?"

"Wherever I wanted," he replied, an edge to his voice. She wouldn't get any unnecessary information from him. He might lead her through Hauke, but he'd set her loose in Arbenia or Vasberg, somewhere they'd never have to cross paths with each other again.

"You just"—her voice hitched high—"*wander*?" She abruptly stopped, something akin to horror on her face.

He found it oddly cathartic. "You've married a *wandering minstrel*, Highness."

"But . . . that means . . ." Her eyes lost their focus, her attention flitting first toward the street and then away. "I can't . . . I can't just *wander*."

"Maybe you should've picked a husband from your own class, then," he callously said.

Her gaze jerked up, her expression unreadable and her breath short in her lungs. Before she could respond, a clatter sounded further up the road. Three horsemen appeared from around a corner. One continued onward while the other two turned, one toward them and the other away.

Thorben swore beneath his breath. Had Marco sent guards to find him?

The rider approaching saw the pair standing beneath an overhang. He raised a small horn to his lips and blasted a short note. The rider further up the street veered around to head their way as well.

That was not a Haukien signal. This had to be an Elisian patrol.

As the horseman drew alongside them, Leonie stepped instinctively closer to Thorben, then away again with a perturbed glance. True to his suspicions, the rider wore the gear of an Elisian soldier. He pushed up his visor, relief in his eyes as he ducked his head in greeting. "Your Highness, the Duke of Ursinbau charged us to find you."

"You must be mistaken," Leonie dryly said. "I'm only a poor beggar woman."

The man shifted in his saddle, rueful as he considered his options. Tonelessly he said, "Then, as a beggar, you're under arrest and have to come with us."

"Nice work," said Thorben to the princess.

She rolled her eyes. "Simon won't do anything. To me, anyway." She stepped forward as the guard dismounted, accepting his assistance into the saddle he had just vacated. The second rider arrived in time to act as escort, grasping her horse's reins.

It was the perfect opportunity for Thorben to melt into oblivion. The beggar Tor could disappear into the storm, the King of Hauke could return to his embassy, and the Duke of Ursinbau could tend to his discarded cousin.

It would have been perfect, that is, had not the dismounted guard grabbed his elbow and tugged him along, a prisoner with his new bride.

CHAPTER 6

The Duke of Ursinbau's home stood tall and stately behind a high stone wall. The guards escorted Thorben and Leonie through a lovely, sodden garden to the broad front door.

"We should probably keep our coverings," Leonie said to the butler who tried to collect her cloak. "I imagine beggars don't trust others with their belongings, for fear they won't get them back."

When she looked to Thorben for confirmation, he clenched his teeth and averted his gaze. The guards motioned them into a sitting room. One remained in the door while the other left the house.

Ursinbau himself was not home, likely combing the streets of Felstark along with his men.

Leonie pushed back her hood and went to warm her hands at the crackling fire. Thorben chose the farthest, most shadowed corner of the room to stand.

If the duke recognized him, that was the end of everything. He might explain himself until his voice ran hoarse, but Leonie would still discover that her mocked and derided suitor had returned.

The story would spread that King Thrushbeard had claimed a bride who did not want him, and he truly would become a source of derision for the whole of Felstark, the whole of Elisia, perhaps even the whole of the Twelve Kingdoms, including his own.

A wiser man would've confessed immediately outside the castle and taken her to the embassy instead.

They passed a silent quarter hour before a commotion sounded at the front of the house. The Duke of Ursinbau, dripping with rainwater, strode into the sitting room and straight to his cousin. "Leonie, thank heavens!" He grasped her hands and stepped back a pace to regard her. "I'm so sorry. The men I posted took refuge in the storm. Are you all right?"

"Perfectly so. Should you like to meet my husband? He's hiding in the corner."

Thorben straightened as she gestured to him, his scowl darkening at her choice of words. The duke glanced irritably his way but returned his attention to the princess. "I'll deal with him shortly. Are you sure you're unharmed?"

"It's only been an hour since the ceremony. What did you think might happen to me?"

He growled but dropped her hands. When he pivoted toward the far corner, Thorben braced himself. Halfway across the room, the duke stopped dead in his tracks.

Recognition flashed into his eyes, and his lips parted.

Thorben, locking gazes with the man, minutely shook his head, hopeful that the duke might accept such an imperious cue to remain silent.

"What's wrong?" Leonie said, ambling cluelessly to her cousin's side.

Ursinbau swallowed and, with a strangled voice, asked, "What's your name?"

A knot loosened around Thorben's heart. "Tor."

"It's short for 'dictator,'" Leonie chirped.

"Not 'suitor'?" the duke wryly asked.

Thorben bared his teeth. "Never."

Ursinbau huffed in frustration and raked his fingers through his dark, damp hair. "Leonie, you'll stay here tonight. I've already ordered a room prepared. Let me escort you to Naira, and she'll take care of you."

The princess frowned, peering from one man to the other. "What about Tor?"

A muscle clenched along the duke's jaw. "Oh, he and I are going to have a *very* long talk." He punctuated this with a stern glare at Thorben, then he ushered Leonie from the room.

The door shut, the guard posted outside now instead of within the doorframe. Nerves jittering, Thorben settled on a leather couch. This was where the international politics began. How would Ursinbau approach a foreign king? What would he demand, and what would he be willing to concede?

When the duke finally returned, closing the door behind him, his expression was unreadable. "Your Majesty," he said, as though the words were ashes in his mouth.

Thorben stood, meeting his accusatory stare. "It's not a legal marriage. It can't be. The priest didn't even ask our consent."

"The King of Elisia can arrange his subjects' marriages. It's an old law, but it's still on the books."

"I'm not one of his subjects."

Ursinbau's self-restraint broke. "Then why did you not identify yourself?"

"Oh, certainly. 'Sorry, King Eustis. I can't marry your daughter because I'm one of the men you invited here for that express purpose.' We got lost, all right? The storm broke, we lost our way back to the embassy, we paused under a porch to get our bearings, and the servants found us and invited us in. I didn't know it was the castle. If I had, I'd've bolted straight into the downpour rather than cross that cursed threshold."

"You expect me to believe that? You just happened to appear as a beggar on the king's doorstep after overhearing his rash oath?"

"Have you met his shrew of a daughter?" Thorben flung one hand toward the shut door she'd vanished behind. "I'd sooner marry a rabid boar!"

The duke staggered back, running a palm down his face as he collected his thoughts. "Then you don't intend to tell Leonie the truth?"

"Not if I can possibly avoid it."

Silence possessed the man. He dropped into a chair by the fire, gaze unfocused and brows furrowed. "This could be construed as an act of war," he finally said.

"On both sides. You think I enjoyed having my exit blocked while a foreign king forced me to marry? And mere weeks before my official coronation, I might add, which *my* people will find most scheming."

Ursinbau swore. "But the marriage stands in Elisia. You didn't identify yourself to prevent it."

"It wouldn't stand in Hauke. No one can force a king to take a wife against his will."

"And you'll risk your treaties with us to nullify it?" A dangerous edge touched the duke's words. He was not Elisia's ruler, but he was next in line for the throne. If King Eustis died tomorrow, Thorben's life would be infinitely more difficult.

"You know it's a sham," the young king said.

"My concern is for Leonie. What do you intend to do with her?"

He huffed a laugh. "Once my advisors confirm that no legal ties exist, I'll turn her loose to run feral where she pleases—preferably not in my kingdom. She doesn't want to be married, Ursinbau. She'll be ecstatic to learn she's free."

"You . . ." The duke paused, perhaps thinking better of the words on his tongue. "You don't know what you're talking about."

Thorben scowled. "She told me so herself, and she certainly made it known at her father's gathering."

"So you'll leave her to beg while you return to your golden tower? And you expect Elisia to countenance this?"

"Forgive me, but Elisia's the one that cast her into the streets."

Ursinbau rubbed his eyes, seeming suddenly decades older. "I tried to prevent this. I did everything in my power. That a foreign king skirted past my efforts and now wipes his hands of any consequences—!"

The unspoken accusation raked across Thorben's sense of right and wrong. "What would you have me do? Accept a marriage neither of us wants?"

"The world is cruel to a woman on her own. You cannot consign Leonie to that fate."

"She consigns herself! She might have married almost any man of her choosing! Alois of Arbenia is practically dying of love for her despite the terrible things she says to him and of him." A sudden thought occurred, stopping him short. "Is there someone she wasn't allowed to choose?"

"What?" Ursinbau asked.

"Is she in love with someone, someone her father wouldn't accept?"

The duke waved aside this possibility. "No. It's nothing like that."

His choice of words caught Thorben's interest. "What is it, then?"

Ursinbau shifted in his chair. "She just didn't want to leave Felstark. This is her home. It's where she's most comfortable. She's still young. It wouldn't have killed her father to delay a few more years, except that—" He broke off, chagrin crossing his face.

"Except that King Eustis wants to remarry, and the bride of his choosing doesn't like Leonie," Thorben finished. At the duke's astonished glance, he grimly laughed. "I have eyes. I saw the interactions between your king and the baroness he invited to greet his guests alongside him." Much as he'd wished to avoid political entanglements, he was already mired. There was nothing left but to plumb the power struggle between King Eustis and his royal heir. "Were you trying to prevent the marriage by keeping Leonie here?"

The duke's eyelids fluttered to half-staff, his whole demeanor signaling his disdain. "I don't care if they marry. I even wish my cousin luck in siring a son, if Amelise of Rotholt can bear him one. She didn't so oblige her last husband, but that's no concern of mine."

"Is it not?" Thorben asked.

A laugh broke from Ursinbau. "My duchy is enough responsibility. I'll ascend if I have to, but ruling a whole kingdom seems like a nuisance. I suppose you know something of that, even if you were raised to the expectation." He wagged a hand, though, dismissing further discussion of this topic. "We're off the beaten path. You're correct that the baroness and Leonie don't get along. They're also too close in age for Amelise's comfort. She wants to be queen, but she doesn't want to play stepmother."

"So she's refusing to marry the king unless his daughter's out from under foot?"

"More or less."

"I suppose I should draft a letter of congratulations when I get home," Thorben blandly said.

"Perhaps you and Leonie can draft it together," said the duke, a fragile glint of hope in his eyes.

"Not happening."

He huffed. "It was worth a try." He sobered, asking again, "What will you do with her?"

Thorben ruminated on this. Tempted though he was to claim no responsibility, his conscience whispered otherwise. "Why can't she stay with you? Tell everyone her beggar husband abandoned her."

The duke's chin dropped in reproof. "And bring such shame upon Elisia's royal house? And upon Hauke's?" he added with a significant stare.

A tiny growl rumbled in the back of Thorben's throat. At last, reluctantly, he said, "I can track down Alois. Maybe after a good spell of begging, Leonie will see the value of his courtship. At the very least, I'm sure he'll be glad to offer her shelter in Arbenia."

"You're supposed to be on a hunting trip with him," said Ursinbau, far too perceptive in his scrutiny. "We all thought you'd left Felstark. Why didn't you?"

The young king averted his eyes, his teeth on edge. "I didn't feel like spending two weeks being called 'Thrushbeard' by my peers."

"So you've been at the embassy this whole time?"

He nodded. "Brooding, as my advisor would say. My brother finally convinced me to get out, to prowl the streets for an afternoon, and this is the result. I should've gone hunting instead."

"She doesn't mean anything malicious by her nicknames," said Ursinbau.

"Then she shouldn't give them so maliciously," Thorben replied.

The duke sent a message to Hauke's embassy, and the messenger brought Marco back with him. Thorben, preemptively steeled against the scolding he was about to receive, listened to his advisor rant for fully half an hour.

"Why does none of this seem to faze you?" Marco finally asked. "You have, through utmost folly, tumbled into a foreign entanglement that could lead us to war!"

Thorben, in resigned repose on the duke's leather couch, merely rolled his eyes. "It won't. There are faults on both sides, and everyone knows it. If we can keep my identity secret from Leonie and Eustis both, no harm will come to Hauke. Ursinbau's not willing to spread the tale that his princess was rejected by a foreign king, and he's not willing to risk my wrath by betraying me to her."

That was the linchpin, the duke's cooperation. He'd agreed that, so long as Leonie ended up somewhere safe, he would not challenge the King of Hauke's handling of the situation. He couldn't, not when his own king had already thrown her out as a beggar.

Marco, though, refused to take an optimistic view. "And what if the laws of Hauke deem the marriage valid?"

"They had better not," said Thorben darkly, "and you'd better not say a word of this to my mother." Queen Julika, having sent him to Elisia as a marriage candidate, would have no qualms about forcing him to keep the alliance regardless of how it had occurred. "Raise the question of a citizen of Hauke forced into marriage with a citizen of Elisia under their antiquated law. You don't have to bring my name into it. You can even say you're advocating on behalf of some poor beggar if you'd like. I'm sure the story of Leonie's downfall will spread fast enough. Meanwhile, everyone will think I'm still off hunting."

"But where will you actually be? You're not staying here in Felstark, are you?"

The young king's face contorted. "No. Ursinbau is going to smuggle us from the city tomorrow, perhaps as far as the border, under pretense of giving his princess a dignified retreat. We'll have to walk to Swifthaven from there. I need you to ride ahead, find some hovel we can live in to keep up this beggar's charade, and send a messenger in search of Alois."

Marco shook his head. "You don't want him involved. If things go sour—if Leonie discovers who you are, or your mother catches wind of any of this—Alois will complicate everything. We already have two kingdoms involved. We don't need a third."

"What else do you propose? Are *you* going to marry her?"

"Don't be ridiculous. We can send her to a convent, if nothing else."

Threat of a convent had driven Leonie to marry a beggar in the first place, but Thorben didn't bother mentioning this. "Don't tell Alois why he's wanted, then. You can encourage him to pass through Swifthaven on his way home instead of taking the crossroads. Tell him I want to apologize for losing my temper, if you must."

"She's not going to marry him. She thinks he's a dullard, remember?"

"A rich, titled dullard," Thorben said. "If her only other option is begging for the rest of her life, I'm sure Alois will look pretty good."

"You're despicable. I hope you realize that. Can you imagine some man pawning off one of your sisters the way you're talking about pawning off your wife?"

Thorben flinched. "Don't call her that. We're not really married. And I can't imagine my sisters behaving with even a shred of the impropriety that Leonie flaunts, so no one should ever have cause to pawn them off."

Marco, thin-lipped, looked away, disapproval rolling off him in waves. In a quiet voice, he asked, "What if you grow fond of her?"

Thorben's conscience twinged. "Impossible."

"But what if? How will you explain the truth?"

"I won't. If I have to ascend as king and annul my own marriage without her ever knowing who I am, I'll do it."

"Regardless of what feelings may develop?"

A small, disbelieving laugh escaped Thorben. "I assure you that my heart is safe, and that Leonie has no heart to speak of. Even if"—he held up a hand to keep his advisor from interrupting—"*if* I somehow set aside my common sense, she does not want to be married. Besides that, she holds the King of Hauke in contempt. If, by some act of bewitchment, I were to fall in love with her, I'd be even more obligated to set her free."

Marco digested this vow, his expression unreadable. "I hope you're right, Tor. I hope this foolish escapade doesn't breed a lifetime of regret."

He took his leave thereafter, armed with instructions for how to proceed. Bert and Gereon were to return to Hauke with him, though the latter would have two weeks of vacation with his family rather than resuming his duties at the castle. Bert's early return could be explained by boredom or annoyance, but

Thorben's mother would know something was wrong if she caught even a glimpse of the valet.

By the time Thorben retired to bed, the night was halfway gone. He sank among too many pillows, the bedchamber far more opulent than a real beggar would have received. The duke intended to ship them off at first light, so resting now was paramount.

Sleep didn't immediately come, though. Instead, the young king muddled over that moment in the kitchen, the power struggle between Leonie and her father.

Had the princess hoped to prevent her father's remarriage? It couldn't be as Ursinbau had said, that she merely wished to remain in Felstark. She might have married half a dozen Elisian nobles and kept a fine house here.

Was the enmity between her and the Baroness Rotholt enough to explain her erratic behavior?

It had to be. Nothing else made sense.

CHAPTER 7

As the first rays of sunlight struck Felstark, a carriage with the duke's crest maneuvered through the gates that separated his house from the street. Thorben, feeling as ragged as his floppy-brimmed hat looked, sank into one corner, watching with bleary eyes as the city slid past his view.

Across from him, Leonie picked at a sugared pastry. Ursinbau's wife had supplied them with food for the journey and extra to carry with them after the coach turned back. As far as Thorben knew, the princess had not questioned where they were going. Instead, she seemed resigned to her fate, quiet in the early morning.

Had she slept any better than him? A careful glance her direction revealed no dark circles beneath her lovely eyes, no signs of fatigue in her posture. Yet, she did not have the same wild energy as the night before.

Perhaps the gravity of her situation had finally sunk its claws into her.

Before they even reached the city gates, he gave up fighting against his exhaustion. He folded his threadbare cloak around himself and curled up on the bench. The jostling carriage lulled his senses, and sleep dragged him into a dreamless abyss.

Hours later, shadows flitted against his eyelids. He opened them to discover a pair of ocean-blue eyes mere inches from his. A yelp cut from his throat. He flung backward, heart racing as he pressed into a corner of the carriage.

Leonie, sitting on the floor between the seats, merely arched an eyebrow.

"What do you think you're doing?" he asked.

"Studying your face," she said. Fear twisted through him—*did she recognize her maligned King Thrushbeard?*—but she continued. "People don't like that sort of thing when they're awake, but I didn't think you'd mind while you slept."

The tension within him eased, though his heartbeat still thundered. "I assure you no one likes it while they're sleeping either. How would you like to wake up to me staring at you so closely?"

She seemed to consider the question but dismissed it almost out of hand. "It's probably different for a woman than a man."

"It's strange either way," he said. "Don't watch people sleep."

Her expression turned winsome. "But you looked so peaceful. How could I resist?" Cynicism tinged her voice. She turned, tipping her face up toward the window opposite him.

They were passing through forest, where sunlight flashed between tall pines. Thorben eased into his seat, observing the scenery. They were on the high pass from Elisia to Hauke, near the crossroads. Leonie's position, huddled next to the carriage wall, seemed almost defensive.

"Why are you still on the floor?" he asked.

She shrugged, maintaining her upward stare. After a long and suffocating silence, she finally said, "A column of riders passed a little while ago. I didn't want to meet their nosy glances through the windows."

That was likely Marco and the rest of the Haukien company. Thorben, relieved to know they had already overtaken him, grunted a laugh. "You didn't want anyone to recognize you?"

She shot him a resentful glare and pushed up to her knees. Under influence of the rocking carriage, she listed but caught herself, shoving away from his bench to drop onto hers. Once settled, she made a show of burrowing backward into her corner, as though to get as far from him as she possibly could.

The Duchess of Ursinbau's food basket shared the bench with her, a red napkin covering its contents. "You haven't eaten anything," Leonie said. "I thought beggars had to take their meals when they could."

Thorben glanced toward the basket. Had she done something to its contents? Taken a bite of everything? Licked it all? Though sleep had restored his hunger, he said, "My appetite has been strangely lacking."

"Did Simon rake you over the coals last night?"

"Is that what he told you?"

She picked at the hem of her sleeve. "No."

Curious, he prodded. "What did he say?"

"That the marriage might not be valid because you're not Elisian by birth."

Why did she seem so unenthusiastic? Thorben frowned. "I'd expect that news to thrill you."

Leonie plastered on a fake smile, meeting his gaze with crinkling eyes and a sarcastic tilt of her head. "Oh, certainly. Nothing could please me more."

"Good. It's my fondest wish to have the marriage annulled before the week is out."

"Then you can return to your wandering, and I can . . . beg in the streets, I suppose."

He steeled his heart against the pangs of his conscience. "Frankly, I don't care what you do."

A laugh broke from her. "Can you truly be so callous?"

He leaned into the space between them, scowling. "You want my pity? You told your father to *horsewhip* me last night."

"If he was going to horsewhip one of us, of course it had to be you," she said. "I only have my good looks. I can't mar them with welts or scars."

"Why you arrogant little—!"

"Are you considered handsome?" she abruptly asked.

This question, on the heels of such carelessness for his wellbeing, made him bristle. "How should I know?"

Leonie looked out the window again. "I suppose beggars don't have mirrors. But surely people would have told you so all your life, if you were. That's all anyone ever says to me."

Did it bother her, everyone fixating on her loveliness? He'd grown a beard because of momentary attention on his chin. What if that were all anyone ever said about him?

His situation had been negative, derisive, though. People only spoke of Leonie's beauty in complimentary terms. "Would you rather be plain?" he asked.

A scoff cut from her, the expression on her face conflicted. "I shouldn't care either way. It seems like a person's behavior should be the better mark of their character."

"I agree. And offering someone else to be horsewhipped is decidedly poor behavior."

She turned to meet his pointed stare, the corners of her enchanting lips faintly upturned. "Then we're equally bad, for you told him to horsewhip me as well."

Thorben snapped his mouth shut. Certainly he had acted in retaliation. But then, what gentleman retaliated against a young woman, regardless of how horrible her behavior? Grudgingly he said, "Fine. We're even."

She hummed a noncommittal sound. Then, "Are you really not going to eat?"

"Why? Did you lick everything while I slept?"

Her laugh, instinctive and inherently charming, caught him off guard. "No, but now I wish I had!" As she reached for the red napkin, he snatched the whole basket away.

After a sour warning glance, he removed the covering. Two loaves of bread and a few pastries nestled within, none looking overly handled.

"Naira thought it might last us a few days. At least as long as it takes us to get where we're going," said Leonie in utmost innocence.

Thorben selected an herb-sprinkled roll and replaced the napkin. As he tore off a piece and chewed, he ruminated over how they would survive until his council could officially void the marriage. Certainly he'd told Marco his plans, but so many details remained. Where would they even sleep tonight? Could he, with the meager funds his advisor had provided him, hire a carriage to take them to Swifthaven, or would they have to walk?

And if he did hire a carriage, would Leonie question his story that he was, in fact, a beggar?

He swallowed, though the crumbs wanted to stick in his throat. They would have to spend at least one night in the elements, or else in a common room.

"What became of your friends?" Leonie suddenly asked. When he frowned, she clarified. "Your fellow musicians, the ones who escaped your awful fate—what will they do with you gone? Will they wander without you?"

"Yes," he said, suddenly grateful that she had hidden when his countrymen had earlier passed. She might have recognized Bert or Gereon in the column of riders otherwise.

Granted, she hadn't recognized Bert last night, but she'd only met him briefly once before that, and in a completely different context. No sense jarring her memories unnecessarily.

"Will you know where to rejoin them? Or will you wander on your own?"

"I don't know," he said, pulling a sizable chunk off his roll. "Why do you ask? Are you having a twinge of conscience?"

"Why should I? None of this is my fault."

He barked a laugh before he could contain it. "Every last shred is your fault! You could be married to an earl or a prince now if you hadn't been so set on insulting everyone." When she gave him an odd look, he covered up his possible blunder. "We've all heard stories of the Laughing Princess who never sees a man but ridicules him. If you're so against marriage, you should have gone to a convent like a proper lady."

A blush rose on her cheeks. "Were those my only choices? Accept a marriage I didn't want or get shut away from the world?"

"Better than being forced to marry a beggar," he retorted. "Do you think I can provide for you the way you've lived before now?"

She eyed his threadbare clothing. "You can barely provide for yourself."

"Right. So you know what that means? Until this is all sorted, you'll have to work. If you want the house cleaned, you'll have to clean it. If you want a meal cooked, you'll have to cook it. If you want money for anything at all, you'll have to earn it."

"Do we have a house?" she asked.

Hardly knowing the situation Marco would engage, he chose the vaguest response possible. "We'll have a roof over our heads. I guarantee you nothing else."

She hugged her arms to her, returning her gaze to the passing scenery, seeming cognizant at last of the gravity of her situation.

Good. Maybe some hard work would humble her. If she was able to earn a few coins, all the better.

———

Near mid-afternoon, the carriage rolled to a halt. As the driver descended to open the door, Leonie tied up the bread loaves in the red napkin, leaving the basket behind. The Duchess of Ursinbau had given her a small bag with an extra dress, of fine make but unadorned and far more practical than the white gown the princess had worn thus far. She added the bundled bread to her sack.

Thorben had nothing but Bert's borrowed pipe, a pocketknife and some coins from Marco, and the clothes on his back. Free of extra baggage, he hopped to the ground and breathed deep the crisp scent of fir trees. They had arrived at the crossroads, a post that pointed five directions, with the same number of paths branching away from it. Ursinbau's carriage wouldn't pass beyond the borderline of Elisia, and Swifthaven was two days' walk from this point, by the road. If they cut through the forest, though, they could arrive sooner.

Wary of encountering someone who might recognize him, Thorben thought leaving the road their best option.

Behind him, Leonie cleared her throat. He turned to discover her waiting within the carriage for help to descend. The driver had crossed around to the horses to inspect their harnesses before his return trip.

"What are you waiting for?" Thorben asked. "Hop down."

A growl rattled in the back of her throat. He watched, amused, as she gingerly stepped into the frame of the door. Instead of toeing for the step or jumping to the earth, though, she grasped either side, rocked backward, and launched herself directly at him.

He yelped as they collided and tumbled to the road. For one breathtaking moment he lay flat, staring up at evergreens and blue sky. Then Leonie swam in his vision as she pushed away.

"Thank you so much for your help," she sweetly said, and she dug her knee into his side for good measure.

He groaned, snatching at her, his fingers catching only air as she danced away from him. "You little shrew," he wheezed, rolling over.

Careless of any injury she had caused, she moved instead to the driver, speaking well wishes for his journey back to Felstark. Thorben climbed to his feet and checked for any sprains or strains, grateful for nothing more severe than a few bruises.

Why did he need to bring her with him? Couldn't his advisors declare the marriage null without both parties present? Couldn't he as king nullify it and send word to Elisia of such? The Duke of Ursinbau should have kept his wretched cousin under his own roof.

Thorben certainly wasn't going to consider her preferences now. With a muttered curse, he started for the crossroads, boots crunching on the gravel. Only after he had passed the sign did Leonie realize he wasn't waiting for her. She yelped and bounded after him, scrabbling steps filling his ears as he continued grimly forward.

She caught up to him at a bend in the road, just as he was descending into the forest underbrush. "What are you doing?" she asked, seizing his elbow.

"I'm going home. The road curves from here. It'll be quicker through the woods." So saying, he shrugged from her grasp and resumed walking.

She glanced fretfully over her shoulder, to the crossroads where the duke's carriage was turning around. After a short sigh, she plunged into the brush, increasing her pace to match Thorben's longer stride.

"What if we get lost this way?" she asked after ten minutes of silence.

"We won't. It's just a matter of heading down. The road has to follow switchbacks along the mountainside, but we can cut straight through."

Sure enough, a couple minutes later, they emerged perpendicular to a long stretch of gravel. Thorben crossed it and reentered the woods on the other side. The forest pitched at a sharper angle. Bracken both clotted their path and promised a cushion should they lose their footing. Wary of Leonie tackling him again, he paused to help her down the steeper sections.

They crossed another stretch of road.

"The switchbacks here take half a day on horseback," Thorben said. "We should be able to reach the bottom within the hour going this way."

"Whose woods are these?" she asked, peering up at the lofty trees.

An impish thought possessed him. "They belong to your King Thrushbeard."

"My—?" Leonie's voice cut short. As her mind caught his words, her whole expression darkened. "Oh. We're in Hauke?"

"Yes. Didn't you see the sign at the crossroads?"

"I was too busy chasing you. Are we staying here or passing through?"

"We're going to Swifthaven. That's where I live."

Her throat rumbled in a tiny, irritated growl.

Thorben, curious, spared her a sidelong glance. "Do you have some complaint against my home country? Or against my king, perhaps?"

"No," she said, though her tone indicated otherwise. Under her breath, she muttered, "Of course you would have to be from Hauke."

He stopped short, arms akimbo as he scowled at her. "What is wrong with Hauke?"

"Nothing," Leonie said, matching his pose, "only I'm sick to death of hearing about it!" She threw her arms in the air and continued her downward march through the woods.

Genuinely intrigued, Thorben scrambled after her. "What have you heard?"

"Oh, about how perfect and lovely it is, and what a delightful situation it would be, and half a dozen more persuasions, until I thought I might vomit. My whole life, my parents tried to convince me of how wonderful Hauke is."

His suspicions about the Elisian king flashed before him anew. "So they did want you to marry—" He cut short before naming himself, chagrin surging within him.

Leonie paused in her descent. "King Thrushbeard? Oh, yes, ever since I was a child. They even tried to arrange it a decade ago. I thought my father would drop it after Mother died, and for a while it seemed he did. As soon as he set eyes on that scheming Amelise of Rotholt, though, suddenly he was sending invitations to every eligible bachelor in the Twelve Kingdoms, and gilding the edges of the invitations to Hauke."

"What's your complaint, though?" Thorben asked. "Why do you despise King—King Thrushbeard so much?"

"I don't despise him. I don't even know him. I just don't want to be the Queen of Hauke—or of anywhere else, for that matter." She pushed onward through a bed of ferns, spine stiff as she walked.

He followed, unable to resist one final dig. "So now you're a beggar's wife instead."

"Which is still preferable to marrying a king."

"You only say that because you don't know how difficult begging can be."

She grunted, as though she disagreed.

Silence filled the space between them. They crossed another stretch of road, and then another after that. Thorben, turning her revelations over and over again, wondered what had set her so against sitting on a foreign throne. Maybe, as Ursinbau had claimed, she really only wanted to stay in Elisia after all.

True to his prediction, they arrived at the mountain's base within the hour. The trees thinned to meadowlands, and a small town spread before them, smoke threading from chimneys into the afternoon sky.

"Is this Swifthaven?" Leonie asked, unimpressed.

Thorben bristled. "No. This is Genneck, barely a way post on the road. Swifthaven is bigger than Felstark."

She shrugged. "I've never been outside Elisia. How far do we have to go?"

"It's another day's walk."

With a sigh, she continued along the gravel, heading straight for the town. Thorben strode past her, cutting into the meadowland, still leery of travelers or countrymen who might recognize their king regardless of his scruffy facial hair.

Leonie shouldered her bag and kept pace beside him. Genneck faded behind fields and copses, the countryside of Hauke opening before them.

When she started to lag, he slowed as well. "Are we not stopping somewhere for the night?" she finally asked. The sun, lowering toward the horizon, swathed her in golden light as though embracing its long-lost sister.

"Do you have money to pay for lodgings?" Thorben asked, already knowing the answer.

A ragged breath rattled through her teeth.

He almost laughed, that such an awful sound could emerge from such a famed beauty, but he forbore from speaking that aloud. Instead, "It's a fine day, not a cloud in the sky. We can curl up in a field beneath a haystack and be perfectly warm for the night. Plus, this way, we can start again at first light."

She didn't answer. They continued from meadows to farmlands, where the hay crops lay in newly threshed heaps. As dusk darkened into night, Thorben picked a likely stack in a remote farmer's field and burrowed them a small nest within it. They ate bread for dinner and curled up beneath the stars.

"Whose field is this, do you think?" she asked.

He'd seen the telltale crest on the fence they'd crossed, part of the reason he'd chosen this location. "King Thrushbeard's. It would be yours too, if you'd married him."

From her stillness, she might have been asleep, but he knew otherwise. Let her ruminate on what she'd scorned. He hadn't wanted to marry her, but it hurt his pride that she'd despised even the thought of him or his kingdom ever since they were children.

It was a blessing that she didn't know she'd married him already. In a way, it was too bad that she never would know. He'd have liked to rub her face in the news after everything was sorted, except that such rude behavior would only invite trouble.

Besides, he was a gentleman, not a boor.

CHAPTER 8

Swifthaven appeared the following afternoon. Traffic along the road increased the closer they drew, prompting Thorben to cut across fields and woods more often. Unlike Felstark, which stood atop its mountain, Swifthaven filled a valley with mountain peaks surrounding it. The tallest still had snow at this time of year, threads of white gleaming against granite.

Leonie observed the scenery in stoic silence, neither praising nor condemning it. For Thorben, though, the mere sight of his beloved mountains restored some of his equilibrium.

Much as he longed to march straight to the castle at the city center, and to the comfort of his own bed, he focused instead on finding Marco. The advisor had agreed to lead him, surreptitiously, to the hovel that would serve as their home, but they had spoken only of the general area to meet, not specifically where or when.

With great relief did he discern him as they passed through the marketplace. His friend, dressed in common attire, leaned against a shop, scanning the crowds headed inward from the city gates. When their eyes connected, Marco wordlessly turned and walked up the street.

Heartened, Thorben followed. Leonie caught his arm.

"What?" he said, frowning at her.

"Don't walk too fast. I'll get lost."

She seemed on edge in such a crowd, her eyes flitting first one direction and then another as though she could not comprehend the scene before her.

It was only the citizens of Swifthaven making their last purchases for the day. But, he supposed, to her it was a foreign city where she knew no one and no one knew her.

With an ounce of pity, he tucked her arm more firmly in his. "Don't let go and you won't get lost."

Marco, instead of continuing up the street, had paused to wait for them. Thorben glanced self-consciously to the princess. Would she notice that they were following someone else? While her gaze was elsewhere, he tipped his chin, motioning for his advisor to go.

They left the market behind soon enough. Leonie, too busy observing her surroundings, never noticed the dark cloak twenty paces ahead of them, that they turned wherever he turned or paused whenever he paused. The condition of the buildings deteriorated, and the smell of too many people in too small of a space pressed upon them. Grime crawled up every wall. Children ran through the streets unattended and mangy dogs scavenged in alleyways.

Thorben had never seen this part of Swifthaven, had never known that such poverty existed within his own kingdom, let alone within the capital itself. When Marco paused beside the door of a mean little hut, twisting a key into its lock with a significant glance over his shoulder, the young king's insides churned.

Perhaps he should have taken Leonie to the castle after all.

But the die was already cast. Marco left the key upon the threshold and continued up the street, to a small tavern, making eye contact just before he went inside.

Thorben squared his shoulders and marched Leonie straight to the hovel.

They paused together outside, surveying the ramshackle structure. "Whose house is this?" she asked in a small, trembling voice, as though fearful of the response.

"Mine," he callously said, "and now yours, until we can get ourselves untangled from one another."

She swallowed and nodded.

He drew her forward and pushed the door open. He had to stoop to cross inside, treading on the key Marco had left behind as he went. Within was a single room, barren but tidy. Beside a straw mattress in one corner stood an empty basin and pitcher. Opposite was a hearth with wood stacked for fuel and a pot angled over its cold, charred grate.

Leonie's breath left her in a whoosh as she surveyed the meager dwelling.

"This is home," said Thorben, a bit too cheerfully. "You stay here and start the fire. I'll be back shortly."

Before he could fully turn, she clamped her hands around his wrist. "Where are you going?"

Startled by the sudden apprehension that gleamed in her eyes, he floundered for an excuse. "To . . . to check in with the neighbors, see if anything important has happened since I've been abroad. Did you want to come?"

She winced and backed away. With shaking voice she asked, "You won't be gone long?"

"No. Just light the fire. There's wood there, and probably some flints."

As she glanced that direction, he stooped to collect the house key and stepped back onto the rubbish-strewn street, shutting the door behind him. It was, perhaps, unkind to leave her in such a place immediately upon their arrival, but he was exhausted after walking all day. If he didn't go after Marco now, he wouldn't have energy to do it later.

Dusk was almost upon them. The tavern was quickly filling with customers who wanted to end their day with a drink and a hot meal. Marco had found a table by the far wall, where he could watch the entrance, and he beckoned as soon as Thorben crossed the threshold.

Thorben wove between patrons to reach him. "The house is perfect," he said as he settled in the opposite chair. "After a week there, she'll be desperate to live anywhere else, preferably as far away from Hauke as she can get."

Marco tipped his head. "I take it the journey did not ameliorate her to you?"

A scoff escaped the monarch's lips. "She hates the whole kingdom—not just me, but all of Hauke."

"Why?"

"It seems her parents harassed her about marrying me since we were children."

"If your parents had done the same, you'd probably hate Elisia. You already dislike it merely because the people there always butcher your name."

He conceded this point. If his parents had ever considered a marriage alliance between him and Leonie, they'd had sense enough not to speak of it to him. His mother was at least open to the idea, given that she'd badgered him to attend the choosing party.

But then, she'd be happy with him betrothed to anyone at all. She didn't like a king ascending without a queen to rule beside him.

"What's happened at the castle since you got back?"

Marco huffed. "Given that I spent most of today leasing and preparing that hovel you're going to live in, nothing much has happened at all. Your mother received us this morning with suspicion. Bert duly reported his boredom, and I gave my excuses that you had sent me to bring him back safely. I'm not sure she believed that."

"You didn't mention anything about a foreign marriage?" Thorben asked.

"I mentioned that one of our people had encountered trouble in Felstark, and that they had appealed to the embassy for help. I thought it best to give as little information as possible until you were back in town. Tor, have you considered what will happen if word gets out that you're living together with a beautiful young woman?"

He straightened in his chair. "It had better *not* get out."

"What if someone recognizes you? I know you look different with the beard, but you're not *that* different to anyone who's seen you more than a few times."

"Which isn't likely in this quarter of the city."

The advisor shook his head. "Talk like that seems to invite the unlikely. I suggest you keep out of sight as much as possible, you and Leonie both."

Thorben grimly chuckled. "Not sure that's possible. I told her she'd have to get a job. She's supposed to be laying the fire right now."

"Does she know how to do that?"

He hadn't bothered to ask. Nor had he even wondered. "How hard is it to lay a fire? My father taught me when I was nine."

"Did her father teach her, though? I think you'll find a Princess of Elisia receives quite a different education than a Prince of Hauke." When Thorben remained unconcerned, Marco rocked back in his chair, folding his arms, disapproval pulling at one corner of his mouth. "You know if she burns the hovel down, you'll owe your landlord a pretty sum—one that won't be so easy to hide from your mother when you withdraw it from the treasury."

"That hut cannot be worth more than two gold," said Thorben.

"It's not the hut itself. It's the location, and the cost to build a new structure, and the rent money he loses in the interim. He can petition the court to force all these fines onto his negligent renters: you and your lovely wife."

With a growl the young king stood. "I've told you not to call her that."

"Until the marriage is annulled, that's what she is. You need to be kinder to her."

Marco was serious. Thorben, irritated by the guilt that pricked him, said, "She'll receive as she gives."

"You know what they say: an eye for an eye makes the whole world blind."

Why did his friend always have a pithy response? It was a good trait in a king's advisor, to speak his mind rather than what he thought his monarch wanted to hear, but sometimes it made Thorben want to punch him.

The pair of men left the tavern together in falling darkness and, after agreeing to meet again the next day, parted ways in the street. Thorben mulled over the conversation as he returned with lagging footsteps to the hovel.

It wasn't on fire. In fact, no light whatsoever shone through the oilskin that covered the single window, nor the crack between the front door and its threshold. With a frown, he pushed open the door.

Shadows met his gaze, no fire in the hearth, no movement in the single room. His heart spasmed. Had she left? Was she wandering the streets of Swifthaven?

What if she decided to present herself to the castle, claiming quarters there as a visiting royal?

"Hello?" he called, striding into the room. "Leonie?"

A hitching inhale sounded from the corner, from the nook on the other side of the bed. "Tor? Is that you?"

His breath left his lungs in a huff, relief and irritation warring within him. "Who else would it be? What are you doing over there? Why haven't you lit a fire?"

"I—" Again that hitching inhale.

Horror descended upon him. Was she *crying*? As his eyes adjusted to the gloom, he crossed around the bed to find her huddled in a ball, her head on her knees and her pale hair like a curtain covering her face from sight.

Awkwardly he knelt, uncertain what to do. "Did you . . . did you not find any flints?"

She didn't reply. She didn't even look up. Smothering yet another wave of guilt, he spun away, crossing to the hearth. Wood lay upon the grate, haphazardly piled as though dumped there, with no consideration for sticks or kindling or how the flames might catch and spread.

Grumbling under his breath, he removed every last piece and started stacking anew. Either Marco or the landlord had left them a flint, as he'd hoped. He struck his pocketknife against it. The sparks caught the twigs and shavings that nested at the bottom of the pile, and light blossomed across the tiny room.

Most of the smoke went up the chimney—a blessing, for he had not the first clue how to clear a blockage there. He nursed the fledgling fire until certain it could sustain itself. Only then did he shift his attention to the corner of the room.

Leonie had raised her head. Orange light reflected off the shimmering tracks on her cheeks.

Thorben steeled his heart against the compassion that instinctively swelled within him. "Why didn't you say you don't know how to lay a fire?"

"You didn't give me a chance. You just tossed me in here and left, and anyone in the world might have walked through that door instead of you."

He brushed aside this hyperbolical fear. "And you could have laughed them right back out again. Isn't that your special skill?"

With a cry of outrage, she yanked a boot from her foot and threw it at him. He instinctively ducked, but it flew wide of its mark. As it clattered against the wall, he gaped at her.

"You are *horrible*," Leonie said, tugging at the laces of her other boot. "Horrible! I should have picked the convent instead."

Thorben, bewildered, said, "Are you only *now* realizing that?"

The second boot sailed through the air, closer to him but still in no danger of striking. He maintained eye contact with Leonie, both of them scowling until her expression crumpled. With a wrenching sob she buried her face in her hands.

It was no good to lay the blame of their predicament at her doorstep. Nor could he take refuge in her former derision of him. He had dreamed that she might one day be toppled from her lofty perch, but actually seeing it happen gave him no satisfaction.

He uttered a self-condemnatory curse and crawled across the space between them. Tentatively, he touched the top of her head. Her trembling immediately ceased, her weeping caught in her throat and her muscles tense.

"I'm sorry," he quietly said. "Neither of us wanted this. I don't know how to treat a wife, and certainly not a wife like you."

She batted his hand away, raising fierce eyes to meet his stare. Even an hour ago he would have read that expression as hostile, a declaration of war.

Now, he saw only vulnerability, and it cut him to the quick. She was like an injured porcupine, in need of help but dangerous to handle. He eased back from her, Marco's call for kindness ringing in his ears.

"We still have a bit of bread left," he said. "Come eat. You'll feel better."

Then he withdrew, daring to rummage in her sack for the last of the food they'd received in Elisia. With nowhere but the bed to sit, he settled in front of the fire and tore the end of the loaf in two.

Clothing rustled behind him. As he took his first bite, Leonie joined him, sitting next to him. He didn't even glance at her as he proffered her portion of bread. She plucked it from his hand and ate in silence.

When at last he thought it safe to speak, he turned to look at her. She was cross-legged, and the socked foot poking out from beneath her skirt caught his attention.

More specifically, the dark stain that blotted the toe.

"Is that blood?" he asked, stooping. She twitched her hemline to cover her foot, but not before he registered the rust color of the splotch and the stiffness it gave her sock. He frowned up at her. "Leonie?"

She clenched her jaw. "The boots. They didn't fit right."

His breath left his lungs. "You walked on blisters until they burst? Why did you not say something?"

"Why would I? Could you have hired a carriage or a horse?" A spark of mockery lit her eyes. "Or offered to carry me instead?"

"We could have taken a slower pace, or at least gotten you some thicker socks. Your feet will need cleaning and bandaging."

She scoffed, derisive. "We don't even have water in the pitcher here."

He pushed from the floor. "I'll find some, and—"

Lightning-quick she caught his hand, forestalling him. "Don't leave again. Not tonight, please."

Again that vulnerability, but this time her expression held pleading instead of rancor. He sank back to his knees, suddenly aware of how easy it would be to fall in love with her. If she looked at him like that always, he could readily worship the ground she walked on.

He was as much of a dullard as Alois. Shaking his head to clear it, he glanced around the room. "We can rest now and get the things we need tomorrow. Hopefully your feet won't become infected during the night."

She still held his hand, an odd tension hovering around her.

It terrified Thorben. He wanted nothing more than to escape, to reorient his thoughts. Surely she was bewitched to overwhelm his senses with so little effort.

"You take the bed," he said, his voice faint. "I'll sleep by the fire, keep it going through the night."

This seemed to be the instruction she sought. With a quick nod, she dropped her hold on him and withdrew. He made a show of wrapping his tattered cloak around himself, of resting with his back to her. The bed creaked as she climbed onto it. Her breathing eventually evened, stillness infusing the tiny room.

Though exhausted, he lay awake for more than an hour. The image of her huddled in the corner, tear-streaked and glowering at him would not leave his mind.

Much as he wanted to believe his own innocence in everything that had transpired between them, he wanted even more never to see such anguish on her face again.

CHAPTER 9

Dawn brought a new set of challenges. He awoke with creaking bones and muscles sore from sleeping on the hard, uneven floor. Leonie, curled tight on the bed, had swollen eyelids and remnants of tears on her cheeks. Her hair, unbound, tumbled around her in a mess.

Somehow, she was still breathtaking.

Conscious not to be caught staring while she slept, he stirred the coals in the hearth and added more wood to the fire. Quietly he pulled on his boots, intending to fetch water and perhaps something they could eat for breakfast. The instant he grasped the door latch, though, Leonie shot upright, eyes wide and wild.

"Where are you going?"

"Just—we need water and food."

She flung from the bed, searching for her boots. "Wait. I'll come with you."

"You don't have to—"

"I need to know where things are, don't I? If I want water, I have to know where to fetch it. Please, just—" She cut off with a hiss as she jammed one bloodied sock into her footwear.

"You shouldn't be walking before we treat your blisters," Thorben said, but she shot him such a black look that he abandoned any other protests. Her white gown had acquired a decidedly dingy cast to it after three days of travel. He'd expected she might like some privacy to change into the Duchess of Ursinbau's gifted dress while he was gone, but she seemed not to care about the state of her clothes as long as she could leave the hovel with him.

Granted, when compared with his threadbare attire, hers was still in excellent shape. Anyone observing the couple would mark her as higher class and likely assume he was her servant.

"I'm ready," she said, straightening her cloak upon her shoulders. She stamped her feet, as though to test how much the blisters might hurt, then crossed the space between them.

Thorben, beside the door, went rigid as she wrapped her arms tight around his elbow. When they stepped out onto the street, she kept to him like a bur stuck to his shirt.

The neighborhood fountain burbled a block away from their hut. They took turns drinking and washing face and hands in its stream, garnering strange looks from the locals coming to collect their day's water. Leonie actually laughed, batting droplets at him when they finally moved on in their quest for supplies.

"Shall we try the market?" he asked. "It might be nice to have something other than bread."

Her stiffness returned. "Do you have any money?"

He slipped his hand into his pocket, rubbing fingers against the silver and copper coins Marco had given him. "Enough for a meal and a few other necessities."

"How are we to earn more?"

He shrugged. "I can play my pipe. You can . . . What can you do?"

She looked forward, mouth flattening. "I don't know. What do women do to earn money in Swifthaven?"

The market lay up ahead, open-air stalls and shops already busy with their early morning customers. Thorben motioned to a nearby booth. "That woman is selling baskets."

"Where did she get them?" Leonie asked.

"I'm sure she wove them herself." They paused to look at the wares, inspecting the baskets beneath the seller's eagle eyes.

"These are beautiful," Leonie said to the woman. "Are they difficult to make?"

The severe features softened. "No, love. It's as easy as breathing. There are plenty of reeds along the river, and no one cares if I cut them."

Thorben, recognizing Leonie's interest, selected the smallest basket—barely large enough to hold a single plum—and purchased it for a copper coin. As they continued along the stalls, he said, "Now you have an example to work off of if you want to try that trade."

She played with it, turning it first one way and then another while they walked. A fruit vendor caught his eyes and he stopped to inspect the produce. Leonie walked on, oblivious, still toying with the tiny basket. He selected two apricots and a few early gooseberries, but as he exchanged coins for fruit, an agonized gasp cut across the market.

He whirled. Leonie, stock-still a dozen yards away, swiveled her head, searching for him.

"Thanks," he told the fruit vendor, expecting the princess to retrace her steps. When she took a stilted step in the opposite direction, he jogged quickly to her. "Hey, I'm right here."

She spun, blinked up at him like someone with too much sunlight in their eyes, and promptly shoved his arm. "I told you not to leave me."

He gestured behind him. "I just stopped to buy some fruit. You're the one who kept walking."

Nonsensically, she clamped onto his arm and twisted them both around. "Let's go home. This was enough for today."

Though he allowed her to lead him, he said, "It's not enough. We can't survive on a pair of apricots."

She kept her attention forward, her chin lifted, and did not respond. For all her indignant bravado, though, the hand on his arm trembled.

"Should we go to the river instead?" he quietly asked. "We can collect some reeds, and then you can stay home and work with them while I gather the other supplies we need."

Reluctantly she nodded. With her face in profile, he could see the pulse fluttering in her neck.

Interesting. Getting lost in the market scared her more than getting left home alone. He tucked this information away, curious at her strong reaction to such a quick and harmless moment.

The tranquil process of gathering reeds restored her equilibrium. Thorben took off his boots and rolled his trousers, wading into the river, cutting canes with his pocketknife and delivering them to her on the shore. When she had a decent bundle, they returned to the hovel. He ducked out to fill their pitcher and pot with water from the nearby fountain. When he reentered, she was already sorting reeds by size, laying them out across the floor.

Heartened, he left her to the task. On pretense of busking, he carried his pipe with him. As he retraced their earlier path to the market, he realized he didn't know what they actually needed, nor how to use most of the supplies he might purchase. He didn't know how to cook, and Leonie wouldn't either.

Bread and milk would have to suffice. In addition to that, he bought some ointment for Leonie's blisters and some bandages to bind the sore spots on her feet.

Silently he prayed for Marco to expedite the marriage nullification. He couldn't send the Elisian princess off into the world on her own—the past two days had proved that much. Once rid of her beggar husband, though, she might petition one of the noble houses of Hauke to shelter her while Marco arranged transportation for wherever she chose to go. She certainly didn't belong in the slums of Swifthaven.

Perhaps Marco's own father might house her. The winsome Ilsebeth would welcome such a spectacle, so long as Bert steered clear until Leonie was gone.

Thorben lingered in the market, playing his pipe on a corner, collecting copper coins in his floppy-brimmed hat. Contrary to Marco's fears, no one recognized their king in their midst. The anonymity was liberating. As morning shifted into afternoon and the crowds thinned, he pocketed his earnings, gathered his parcels, and headed home.

When he opened the hovel door, Leonie looked up from the floor like a startled roe.

All the reeds lay around her in shambles, shattered and jagged.

After a breath of silence, she said, "They kept breaking when I tried to bend them."

His heart sank. Carefully he set aside the parcels and crouched before her, pulling at the hands she held to her chest.

Bruises and angry cuts marked her palms. He dragged his eyes from the sight to meet her wide gaze, conscious of the shallowness of her breath.

"I think you have to soak the reeds first to soften them," he gently said.

"I didn't know." She blinked and pulled one hand away to wipe her gathering tears.

Thorben, his conscience twinging, turned back to the parcels by the door. "I bought a salve for your feet. We can use it for your hands as well."

She sniffled. "How did you pay for it?"

"I played my pipe in the market."

"Is that why you were gone so long?"

"Yes. Were you worried?"

"Of course not." The haughty tip of her nose belied the trembling in her voice. He sighed and tended to first her hands and then her feet, grateful that he had remembered to buy those necessary supplies. Her left foot had more blisters than the right, clustered mostly on her heel, all of them burst and the skin angry. He wrapped the bandage carefully and fit her sock back around it to hold it in place.

The act of service seemed terribly intimate—so much so that he was surprised she allowed it. Thankfully, she remained silent throughout, her attention fixed upon the fireplace.

When he finished, he sat back on his haunches and said, "I don't think basket-weaving is the right trade for you."

A huff of laughter broke through her melancholy. "What am I to do, then?"

Frowning, he cast his mind upon skills a princess might already have. His mother and sisters spent a ridiculous amount of time in needlework. "What about spinning thread?"

Leonie looked dubious. "Where would we get the spindle and the fibers?"

Heartened that she at least knew what implements the trade required, he said, "I'll go buy them. I should have enough money."

She bit the inside of her cheek, as though stopping a protest from leaving her tongue, and mutely nodded. Before she could change her mind, he left the house again.

Obviously she didn't want his monetary help—and little wonder. He'd already impressed upon her his poverty, and they were supposed to part ways as soon as their sham of a marriage dissolved. She wouldn't want to incur a debt with someone determined to abandon her.

An unbidden sense of responsibility spurred him, though. He found a narrow textiles shop a couple streets over. There he purchased a drop spindle, a small distaff, and some raw flax. His mother and sisters had always enjoyed spinning and coloring their own thread. While he had not the first clue about dyes, the flax would provide Leonie a decent starting point.

"You know how to do this?" he asked when he presented her with his purchases.

She'd swept the broken reeds aside while he was gone, though bits and pieces still littered the uneven stone floor. Distractedly, she nodded. "My mother used to spin her own thread."

"Then I can leave you to it?" he asked, conscious that Marco would be wandering through the neighborhood soon. When she looked up sharply, he created an excuse for his absence. "I still have to register a formal petition for the annulment."

"Oh. Yes, go." She waved him toward the door.

He paused on the threshold, hesitating, but she was already intent upon her task, wrapping the distaff with flax, picking away a wisp of fiber that clung to the bandage around her opposite hand. Whether she could spin thread fine enough to sell, she seemed at least to understand how to begin the craft.

Marco had not arrived yet in the tavern, but Thorben sat at the same table they'd used the previous afternoon and settled in to wait. His advisor appeared within half an hour, with a surge of patrons arriving for their end-of-the-day drinks.

"Tell me you have good news," Thorben said as Marco settled across from him.

"That depends on your definition of good. I brought the issue of a foreign marriage to the king's council. They seemed inclined toward annulment until they discovered that King Eustis himself was involved."

Thorben leaned sharply forward, his voice dropping to a hiss. "You didn't mention my name, did you? Or Leonie's?"

"No," said Marco scornfully. "I'll keep you both out of it as long as possible, but I had to admit the marriage came about through a royal decree. The council has to review all our treaties with Elisia, to gauge whether an annulment would put us in violation and whether that's a risk we want to take. If they knew their own king was ensnared . . ."

But Thorben staunchly shook his head. "Once my name's attached, there's no escaping it."

"How are you and Leonie getting along?"

"I made her cry last night. She's skittish and over-sensitive, and she doesn't know the first thing about basket-weaving." When his advisor arched an eyebrow, he recounted the events since their last meeting, including the shattered reeds. "You would think, after the first few broke, she would realize there was some missing step, but instead she kept trying."

"Some might consider that an admirable trait," Marco dryly said.

"Futile perseverance? Hardly."

"And what's she doing now?"

"Spinning flax into thread. Her mother taught her how. Or at least," he amended with a frown, "she said her mother used to spin her own thread."

Marco propped his elbows on the table, leaning in to ask, "Didn't her mother die when she was still a girl?"

"Yes, but—"

"And you didn't bother staying long enough to check whether she actually knows how to spin?"

"No, but—"

"Tor, you're an idiot." He raised a hand to ward off his monarch's protest. "Maybe she knows exactly what to do, but if so, why wouldn't she propose spinning as her desired trade from the start? Proficient spinners can make an excellent income. Even gentlewomen can do it without tarnishing their reputation: my own sister sometimes spins for extra pin money. So why didn't Leonie propose it before?"

Misgivings churned within Thorben's gut. "Surely she would not pretend to be proficient at something she knows nothing about."

"You know her so well after three days?"

He pushed abruptly from the table, standing, scowling down on his advisor. "Are you trying to worry me?"

Marco wryly smiled as he also stood. "No, only to make you think. I've given you all the news I have. Perhaps we should part ways for tonight."

The sun had not yet set when they left the tavern. Thorben turned the opposite direction of his friend, pretending nonchalance.

When a glance over his shoulder showed Marco rounding a corner, he broke into a run to the hovel down the street.

With the golden light of sunset behind him, he threw open the door, illuminating the small room.

Leonie, standing near the bed, froze. At first glance, she seemed the picture of domestic beauty, a lovely maiden with fiber-laden distaff in one hand and drop-spindle dangling by its thread near her feet.

The thread, though, was mottled with the same rust-colored smears that marred her dress front and stained her hands.

"No, no," Thorben said, surging forward. He pulled the spinning implements from her and tossed them away, his focus on her palms, on the blood smeared across them. The coarse flaxen thread had torn open the cuts from her earlier misadventure with reeds. "Why did you take off your bandages?"

Haltingly she said, "The flax kept sticking."

A glance toward the floor showed her discarded bandages in a pile, with rough, unspun fibers clinging to them like too many burs. He raised his incredulous gaze to her face. "Why did you not stop the moment you started bleeding?"

She spoke faintly, fearfully. "I . . . I was getting the hang of it."

An anguished breath escaped him. He pushed her to sit on the bed then retrieved the ointment and leftover bandages. Much as he wanted to lecture, he held his tongue, instead kneeling before her, cleaning and wrapping her injuries for the second time that day. Thankfully, the damage was not as dire as his initial impression. Just, her skin was pale, and her dress was pale, and the flax was pale, so every fine smear of blood seemed amplified in his moment of panic.

When the last finger had received its salve and bandaging, he gently cradled her hands between his and looked up into her ocean-blue eyes. It took every ounce of his self-restraint to say simply, "I don't think you should pursue any more craftsman's trades."

Leonie studied him as though looking at him for the first time. "Then what am I supposed to do?"

"For now? Rest and heal."

"And when your king grants the annulment? What am I to do then?"

He had no answer. His attention dropped to her hands, to the bandage-wrapped fingers that he suddenly, irrationally wanted to kiss.

Futile perseverance, he had called her efforts. She kept pushing at a task even when she knew she was failing, because the world had given her no other options.

He had given her no other options.

CHAPTER 10

T hat woman is going to send me to an early grave," he told Marco the following afternoon. When he recounted the scene he had returned to, the advisor only shook his head. Thorben huffed. "What fool keeps on spinning when the thread cuts their hands?"

"One who sees it as their only choice," Marco quietly said.

The young king banged his head on the tabletop, the din absorbed by the noise of the tavern around them.

"What's she doing today?"

"Resting. We sat swapping folk tales all morning."

"Sounds horrible."

He raised his eyes to meet his advisor's sardonic gaze. "Sarcasm duly noted. It was difficult keeping her entertained, especially because she's constantly fretting about how she can provide for herself. What am I supposed to do with her?"

"What did she spend her time in Felstark doing? Obviously not needlework or embroidery."

"Nor painting, nor music," said Thorben glumly. "As best I can discover, she used to ride her horse all morning and spend all afternoon reading history books, she and her maid together. I half-wish she'd allowed the woman to come with her, for at least she'd have a companion she actually likes."

"You seem terribly concerned for her welfare, considering how much you despise her," Marco said.

Thorben simply glowered at him and changed the subject. "What has the council discovered in the treaties?"

"Mixed results. We're supposed to honor their laws and contracts, but they're supposed to honor ours as well. Some of the council believes that if their king can decree a marriage without consent, our king should be able to dissolve it without consequence. Others suspect that King Eustis will take deep offense at you blatantly undoing his deeds."

"Bert hasn't confessed to my mother yet, has he?"

Marco chuckled. "Not yet. He's spending most of his days mooning over my sister, though, so Queen Julika readily believes that was his true reason for returning. She is irritated with me for letting you go off with Alois, though. If she catches wind that Gereon is back in town, we're all doomed."

This didn't worry Thorben. The valet knew to steer clear of the castle until summoned. If the council was already half-convinced that he could annul a foreign marriage, perhaps he could be free of this trouble in another day or two.

"But what am I to do with Leonie?" he asked, returning to the subject of his bride's failed attempts at earning money.

"Find her something to sell," Marco said, "something she doesn't have to create herself. If she's only sitting in the marketplace exchanging goods for coins, she shouldn't be able to injure herself, right? So buy her a load of pottery or something, and make her a shopkeeper instead of an artisan."

The idea had merit, but it came with one prominent obstacle. "I don't suppose you have money to lend toward this enterprise," Thorben said.

His advisor grinned. "No, but you do." He plunked a small sack onto the table, the coins within clinking. "I wondered how long before you asked for more funds. I'm shocked you lasted this long."

A scowl descended on the young king's face. "It's only been a few days."

"But you're used to luxury, not scrounging for your next meal. I imagine this has been an eye-opening experience."

He pocketed the sack, nodding. Once his own troubles resolved, and once he officially ascended, he would address his council about the poverty in Swifthaven and how they might better meet the needs of the common citizens.

"You want me to do what?" Leonie stared at the handcart parked in front of the house, at the stacks of glazed bowls and plates and vases piled within its bed.

"You can just sell it. I borrowed money from a friend to buy this cheap. You can set up a place in the market and sell each piece at a higher price. We pay back the loan, and you keep the extra, with no injured fingers involved."

Her breath fluttered, shallow in her lungs. "You want me to sit in the market? What if someone recognizes me?"

Thorben frowned. "In Swifthaven? Do you know a lot of people here?"

"I don't know! What if someone who knows me is traveling here and sees me? And then they come to speak with me and—!" Her voice cut out, her eyes wild as she glanced up and down the street.

He followed her gaze. While many who passed in front of their ramshackle house stared at the beautiful girl beside him, they did so without a shred of recognition. The men admired her pretty face, and the women gazed upon the gown that she wore, the dress gifted to her by the Duchess of Ursinbau. The deep red of its bodice reflected early morning sunlight in flashes of crimson, its fabric finer than any other dress in this district of the city.

"Couldn't you just laugh at them? Or pretend not to know them?"

Leonie shot him a glare that skewered straight through him.

"I suppose, if you'd rather not set up shop," he said reluctantly, "you don't have to. Only, I've already bought the pottery, so I'll have to pay my friend back his loan somehow."

She bit her lower lip, a picture of troubled indecision.

"If you're worried about being recognized, you could try wearing a wimple," said Thorben, mostly in jest. The duchess had included such a garment in her gift, and Leonie had immediately cast it aside.

At its mere mention, her whole body froze. Slowly she looked up, her eyes lacking focus as she gazed upon him. "You mean . . . I could just . . . blend in with everyone?"

He tipped his head, curious at her odd phrasing. "When you don't want people to recognize you, blending in is generally the goal."

"And other people won't recognize me in a wimple?"

"It would hide one of your fairly distinguishing features." He tweaked a lock of her golden hair.

She clapped a hand to her head, a faint blush rising on her cheeks.

Conscious that he might be accused of flirting, he shifted his attention back to the cart full of pottery. "Well? What do you think?"

"Will you be there with me?"

"Long enough to help you set up. I think people are more likely to buy from you if I'm not hovering."

Misgivings crossed her face, but she schooled them away. "All right. If you think I can make money doing this, I suppose it's worth a try."

She didn't sound convinced, but he accepted her words rather than acknowledging her doubts. Reluctantly she ducked back into the hovel and emerged again with a snowy white wimple covering her hair.

"How does it look?"

He instantly hated it. Wary of the reason behind this visceral reaction, he spoke an opposite response. "You're as beautiful as ever."

Leonie grimaced, a belated reminder that she didn't like such compliments. But then why had she asked, if not for him to praise her?

Before he could question this aloud, she said, "Let's go while there's still time left in the day to sell anything."

The sun hadn't even been up an hour. He moved toward the cart handles, but she stepped into place before him, waving him off. "If it's my shop and my wares, I should be responsible for it."

"If you raise blisters on your hands in addition to all the cuts and bruises . . ." he replied, letting the conclusion dangle in the air.

But instead of bristling, a spark of sarcastic mischief lit her eyes. "What? You'll rub them with salve and bandage me up again? How truly terrifying."

His heart flip-flopped. He averted his gaze and cleared his throat. "Maybe I'll make you bandage yourself this time."

She huffed a quiet laugh and grasped the cart. It was better made than he should have been able to afford, gliding smoothly along the road as she pulled. He ambled beside her, feeling mostly useless until he noticed the sweat breaking along her brow.

"Are you sure I can't pull that for you?" he asked.

"You won't always be here to do things for me."

The reminder annoyed him, though he did not care to examine why. Instead, he pitched his voice light. "All the more reason to use me while you can."

Leonie paused mid-step, looking up, assessing. After a quiet moment, to his surprise, she rested the cart and withdrew a pace so that he could more easily take the position she had occupied. He grasped the handles and pulled, oddly pleased.

As they approached the market, she drew closer to him, her wary gaze flitting across the murmuring crowds.

"Careful of your skirt," Thorben said when he noticed how close her hemline was to the wheel.

She hopped away, checked the distance, and adjusted her walk accordingly. Every few seconds, her head angled toward him, as though she wanted reassurance that he was still beside her.

Halfway down the first market street, they found a tiny gap between a farmer and a spice merchant. Neither stall owner declined when Leonie, smiling, asked permission to set up between them. Thorben helped her angle the cart into the back of the space and unload her wares onto a blanket.

"Shall I leave you to it?" he asked when she stood among nicely arranged pottery.

Fretfully she peered at him, twisting her fingers. "You'll be nearby?"

He tipped his head up the street. "I'll go play my pipe on the corner. Where you hear the music, that's where I'll be."

She took a deep breath and nodded, shifting her attention to the wares stacked at her feet.

Thorben walked away before he could change his mind. Her nervousness at being left alone in the marketplace wore upon him, but surely she couldn't get hurt selling pottery.

Halfway to his designated corner, he looked back over his shoulder, expecting that she would be watching his retreat.

She'd already engaged a customer, smiling, laughing, looking as though she belonged with the other merchants that lined the road. The wimple did make her blend in as intended, but in a way that dampened her ethereal charm. She looked grounded, sensible, mature.

After exchanging coins for wares with her customer, she glanced up the street his direction. Her gaze slid right past him, though.

He shook himself from staring and completed his trek to the corner. When he started piping, floppy-brimmed hat on the cobblestones by his feet, he glanced toward Leonie's stall to check that she could hear him.

She already tended another customer, careless of his presence.

She didn't need him after all. This realization stung more than he cared to admit.

***

"Every last piece," he said to Marco that evening, in lieu of a greeting. "She sold every last piece of pottery, and all of it before noon. The minute she donned her famous smile, people flocked to her like ants to a bowl of sugar."

"Men, you mean," said Marco.

Thorben blinked. "What?"

"Men flocked to her, right? Most of her customers were men?"

"I . . . yes."

"You're an idiot," the advisor said. "She's a beautiful young woman with an engaging manner when she wants to please—and sometimes even when she doesn't. Of course men flocked to her. And then they had to buy something in order to impress her. If she sets up shop again, you need to keep better watch. Otherwise, some of these customers might try buying something other than pottery."

The implied meaning did not escape Thorben. He scowled, affronted. "She was wearing a wimple. That marks her as a *married woman.*"

"If you think that stops people, you have a lot to learn about the world. How did she feel about the whole venture?"

"She's pleased beyond words. Bounced the whole way home, with a sack full of coins jingling from her belt." He sprawled against the tavern table, oddly despondent at this development.

True, he had told Leonie to earn her own keep, and her previous attempts had been disasters. He had simply not expected success to this degree. Some of her customers had paid five times the worth of their new vessels.

Which meant that Marco was likely correct, that they were trying to fix Leonie's interests rather than fill out their tableware.

"She must not have called them any names," he grumbled.

"Don't let it rankle you. No one's forcing her to marry any of them, so she has no cause to resort to insults."

This only irritated him more, though. If he had met Leonie without anyone trying to orchestrate a betrothal between them, would she have liked him? Or would she have still called him Thrushbeard and laughed as she spun away? As a beggar he received more attention from her than he had as a prince or a king. She never pretended to like him, but she hadn't branded him with any rude epithets, either.

A small, secret part of him wanted things to remain as they were, with the odd companionship that had sprung up between them.

Thus, he forced himself to ask about the marriage annulment. "Has the council made any decisions?"

"You won't like it," Marco said.

His heart flip-flopped. Had they decided he couldn't annul a decree from King Eustis after all? Were he and Leonie stuck together? And if so, how would he break the news to her?

"Tell me," he said.

"They've agreed that an annulment can be granted."

Dismay snaked through him. He pushed it away, forcing relief into his voice. "Why wouldn't I like that?"

"Because they also agree that you have to be the one to grant it, officially, and only after your coronation so that it has the full weight of your kingship upon it."

His jaw dropped. Marco nodded encouragingly. "B-but . . . the coronation is still three weeks away!"

"Two. You've lost some time while you've been playing vagrant. It's not that long to wait for your precious annulment, but you can't ascend to the throne as a beggar. So, you either have to confess to your wife or else contrive a reason to leave her alone in your hut for a few days and then hope that she doesn't come to watch the coronation."

"I am supposed to be a traveling minstrel," said Thorben with a speculative frown.

Marco swatted the side of his head. "Just tell her the truth. It's going to emerge somehow, and the longer you pretend you're only a beggar, the angrier she'll be when you finally reveal otherwise."

"I don't want her to know."

"It's a miracle she hasn't figured it out already. She already knows you well enough to recognize you without the beard, if not by your face then by your voice and your mannerisms."

This had already occurred to Thorben. "Why would she even go to the coronation, though? She hates King Thrushbeard."

His advisor tutted. "You're only tempting fate at this point. I'm willing to bet that she'll be just as mortified as you are when she learns she's married to the King of Hauke."

Thorben silently agreed, and that was his biggest problem. More than anything, he wanted to avoid the disdain Leonie would express should she ever learn his true identity.

CHAPTER 11

Thorben didn't meet with Marco again for a few days, having no interest in further pressure to confess. Despite her success in the market—or perhaps because of it—Leonie expressed reluctance to set up shop again, so he didn't have to worry about customers plying her for more than pottery, either.

Instead, they spent their days walking through the lower wards of Swifthaven and along the river. She bought extra socks, a new blanket, even a pad for Thorben to sleep on by the fire—despite his protestations that she should not spend her earnings on him. He often busked so he could chip in for hot meals from street vendors and fresh fruit from the market.

One afternoon she finally splurged on something frivolous: a little bag of seeds to feed the birds.

"Everything about this kingdom reminds me of birds," she said as she tossed a handful across the small plaza they rested in. Their stone bench, sheltered beneath a row of stately elms, afforded them full view of comings and goings within the square. "Even its name sounds like 'hawk,' but with a funny vowel: *Hauke.*"

Thorben, sitting with elbows resting on knees, watched the crows and sparrows fight over their afternoon meal. Swifthaven had received its name from migrating flocks that passed through twice a year. The kingdom's name was coincidence, though, and he couldn't think of any other avian associations but one.

"Is that why you renamed the king to Thrushbeard?"

Leonie stilled, fingers sifting birdseed. "I suppose so," she said, though her voice was wooden.

Curious, he glanced toward her, but she studiously did not meet his gaze.

He returned his attention to the birds, clearing his throat. "Do you still prefer marriage to a beggar over a king?"

"Oh, infinitely." When he recoiled, her delicate laugh pealed out across the square. Bumping shoulders with him, she said, "This hasn't been difficult at all. I think I might actually be good at it."

In answer he caught her wrist, raising her hand where she could see the paper-thin scabs and mottled bruises that lined her fingers and palms. "*This* is preferable to living in luxury?"

She carelessly shook off his hold. "Neither of us knows how King Thrushbeard would treat a wife. Maybe he's horrible."

"You already told me that I'm horrible," Thorben said.

Again she laughed. "So you are. But you don't have a whole horrible household as well. Marrying a king—or a prince, or an earl, or a baronet—involves gaining a hundred new relations."

He bristled, offended on behalf of his mother, his brother, and his sisters. "How do you know they would be horrible?"

"How do you know they wouldn't be?" Leonie countered. "I was my parents' only child and my father still threw me out when I didn't do as he wanted. Why should I expect better treatment from anyone else's family when my own found me expendable?"

A growl rumbled in the back of his throat. "You can't judge the rest of the world based on how your father treated you."

She didn't answer this, instead growing quiet. Another handful of birdseed tumbled across the pavers in front of them, to the sparrows' delight.

Thorben, struck by the idea that his family had posed just as much of a deterrent to Leonie as he himself did, wondered if this drove her rejection of other suitors as well. Alois was a second son, certainly, but he didn't know about others who had courted her hand.

Marco's advice for him to confess rang across his ears. He could never tell her the truth. She would despise him.

With an odd tightening in his chest, he asked, "What do you think about me returning to my travels?"

Leonie stiffened. "I thought . . . I mean, don't you need to stay here, at least until your petition for an annulment is answered?"

"*Our* petition," he said. "You still want it as well, don't you?"

Her shoulders shook with laughter. "When did my opinion factor into any of this? I had no choice in the marriage. I'm not sure why I should have any in its dissolution."

He wanted to press her for her true feelings. If there were any hope for Thorben of Hauke, he would have. But, especially knowing what he did now, annulling the marriage was the only way forward for both of them. So, her opinion didn't actually matter.

"I have every hope the annulment will go through," he said, boxing the conflicted feelings that roiled within him. "My contact with the council says it can't happen until the king returns from his trip, and probably not until after his official coronation. So what do you think about me traveling between now and then?"

A ghostly shiver passed through her, but she pitched her voice light. "Fine. I don't care."

"Leonie," he said sharply.

She didn't glance at him, but a furrow cut between her brows. "I told you I don't care." To punctuate this, she hurled the birdseed—bag and all—across the pavement. It arched through the air, scattering seed upon the crowd of flapping wings and open beaks. Leonie pushed away from the stone bench, striding for the nearest street as though indifferent of whether he followed.

"I think she actually does care," he said to himself, and those conflicted feelings stirred anew within him.

Hadn't Marco warned him against getting attached? And now Thorben knew she would never accept the King of Hauke by choice, and Tor the beggar, of necessity, needed to disappear.

That evening as they ate meat pies bought from a stall in the market, Leonie asked, "Where do I get more pottery?"

Thorben paused, his food halfway to his mouth. "I thought you didn't want to sell again."

"If you're going traveling, and if the annulment is imminent anyway, I don't have much choice. I'm good at it, so I might as well earn more money."

He took a bite and chewed slowly, hating that she had drawn this conclusion—mostly because she was correct. "I bought it from a potter a few streets over."

"Can you take me with you to get another load?"

The pie suddenly tasted like ash in his mouth. He nodded, his gaze unfocused. Mentally he chastised himself: an independent Leonie was no longer his concern. He *wanted* to clip any strings between them, to set her free, and all the better if he could do so knowing she had the skills to take care of her own needs.

At some point over the past week, though, despite her sharp edges, she had somehow burrowed deep into his heart and nested there now.

Hadn't he sworn to forsake her if this very situation occurred? "We can go first thing in the morning," he said.

When he curled up on the hearthstones that night, wrapped in his tattered cloak and lying atop the thin pad she had insisted on buying him, he secretly wished that dawn would never come.

But come it did, and all too soon. They trekked to the potter's kiln three streets away, pulling the handcart with them. Leonie, at her winsome best, haggled with the potter for the wares she wanted.

It cost her every last coin she had left, but if her skill as a pottery merchant ran true, she would be penniless only a few hours.

She allowed Thorben to pull the cart as far as their house, only to stop him there. "I'll go alone from here. I have to know how to do everything by myself if you're leaving."

No rancor marred her voice, but the words skewered him all the same. He bit back a response, nodding instead. She pressed on, that cursed wimple covering her glorious hair from the sunlight that streamed around her. He watched until she reached the corner, but she never looked back.

Marco's warning of overly attentive customers played in his ears. As she vanished from sight, he set off after her, determined to watch from afar even if she didn't want him present.

He'd expected her to trek to the same spot as before, between the farmer and the spice merchant. Instead, to his confusion, she paused at the edge of the market, hesitated, then parked her cart near the street corner. As she unfurled the blanket she would use to display her wares, he crept to a different vantage point. Much of the foot traffic wouldn't see her in that location, customers often turning back before they reached the market's end. Only those entering from this side or passing all the way through would encounter her informal stall. Her proximity to the intersecting street created a liability as well: someone rounding the corner too quickly might stumble over her pottery, damaging it.

Maybe she didn't realize. Or maybe she was as wary as Marco for customers soliciting more than a new bowl or plate. Maybe she *wanted* her stall to have less visibility than last time. Thorben ducked into an alley between two shops, a perfect vantage to watch whether anyone accosted the lovely young woman throughout the morning.

Despite her poor location, she still drew plenty of attention. Customers, some blushing and others flirtatious, purchased vessels. One man, beneath the critical gaze of his wife, actually forgot to take his new vase with him after handing over his coins. He came back, stammering, to retrieve it, Leonie laughing and his wife glowering all the while.

The princess-turned-beggar seemed perfectly capable of handling herself. Thorben, snug against the alley wall, told himself that she would be fine on her own.

Horses clattered further up the street. The crowd, mostly on their feet, parted to create a path for the riders. From his tucked position, he could not see much beyond a bobbing hat with a long feather pluming from it. Then—

"Leonie? Leonie, is that you?"

Thorben sat up straight. He moved into a crouch to better see the scene. At the corner stall, Leonie's smile turned brittle.

Alois of Arbenia swung from his horse, pushing past pedestrians as he rushed to the pottery stall. "Leonie, my sweet!"

She stood, but when he tried to grab her hands, she held them to her chest and backed away. In her most mocking tone, she asked. "Do I know you, sir?"

"Oh, how you tease." He stamped one foot, like a child in a snit. "Surely you should take pity on your most ardent and loyal admirer."

Had Alois always been this insufferable? Every instinct in Thorben urged him to launch across the street and tackle the man. Common sense kept his feet planted in the alley.

Leonie's amused expression turned derisive. She gestured to her head-covering. "I don't need admirers, dullard. I'm a married woman now."

He huffed, a theatrical show of indignation. "Your father is the greatest villain alive, and this beggar he forced you on is doubly so! Where is he? I'll teach him a lesson for grasping above his station! Fate itself has brought me to your rescue, fair damsel, and I won't leave until I see you restored to your proper fortune."

Her hands clenched and unclenched. "Kindly continue on your journey, sir. There is nothing for you at this stall."

"Oh, my dear girl," said Alois. He tried to pat her cheek, but she bucked her head away. Conscious of their gathering audience, he retracted his hand with a chuckle. Behind him, his valet and a pair of guards waited, still astride their horses. He glanced toward them and then back to Leonie. "It's insupportable for such beauty to occupy this lowly place. I'll advocate on your behalf." He fished into his pouch for a gold coin. When she refused even to extend her hand, he dropped it into one of her bowls and sauntered back to his horse.

The crowd goggled as he hoisted himself again into his saddle. Once astride, he kissed his fingertips and gestured them toward Leonie.

She remained stoic, no longer the Laughing Princess.

Horse hooves clipped along the cobblestones, passing her stall and continuing up the street.

Thorben, sheltered within the alley, looked from Leonie to Alois, unsure which one to spy on. Leonie, a hard expression on her face, picked up the bowl that contained Alois's gold and swung it so that the coin went flying. It pinged as it hit cobblestones. Someone cried out in joy, claiming their new fortune.

"Pottery for sale," Leonie called, her bright and charming smile in full force.

She would be fine. Any mischief would come from Alois. Thorben, conscious of her glimpsing him, ducked from the alley and bolted after the Prince of Arbenia.

The foreign horsemen had not gone far, easily visible above the foot traffic most predominant in this part of the city. They stopped in front of a public house, dismounting, securing their horses before they entered. As he skirted through the same door, Thorben pulled the floppy brim of his hat lower, the better to obscure his face.

It was only midday, so customers were few in the drinking establishment. Thorben slipped into a chair nearest the door, his back to the Arbenians. Alois had already claimed a booth across the room, but although he leaned close to his travel companions, he made no attempt to conceal his voice.

"The poor girl must be in trauma. Who knows how this brute has been treating her. Selling pottery by the road? Who but a beggar could ever let her stoop so low?"

His valet, with more thought for discretion, said quietly, "Your Highness, we're in Hauke, not Arbenia. We should appeal to the royal family."

Alois scoffed. "I'm not telling *Thrushbeard* that she's here. He'd swoop in and rescue her himself, and then take all the credit for it even though I'm the one who found her! No, if she's too afraid to lead us to her husband, we wait until she packs up her wares. Either the beggar will appear, or we can follow her to where he lives. We'll make short work of him and take Leonie onward with us to Arbenia."

One of his guards cleared his throat uncomfortably. "Your Highness, that might be construed as kidnapping."

"We are *rescuing* her," the prince replied, an edge to his voice. "She'll thank us, I assure you."

Thorben peeked over his shoulder as the pair of guards exchanged a telling glance. They might not like this plan, but they wouldn't fight against it.

Which meant that Leonie needed to be out and away from the market before Alois returned possibly drunk and thus more foolish than usual.

The beggar king slipped out the door again, hands shaking as he started back, but he stopped not ten paces down the street. What was he supposed to do, tell her he'd been watching her? And if she accepted his story, what would happen if Alois appeared while they were packing up all that cursed pottery?

Rashly he retraced his steps, untethering the Prince of Arbenia's horse. He tugged the hood of his tattered cloak up over his head, over his hat, and climbed into the saddle. Heart racing, he spurred the beast, leaning close to its neck, urging it to canter, calling a warning to those in the road.

Pedestrians scattered. Thorben angled the horse to clip the corner of the street as he turned too fast into the market. A shriek sounded in his ears, along with the shattering of pottery. As a path opened before him, he hazarded a glance back over his shoulder.

Leonie hugged the wall, safe and whole, her wares in shambles before her. A ragged sigh of relief escaped him.

He turned at the next corner and rode around the block, back to the same public house he'd stolen the horse from. Alois would never know it had been missing. Thankfully no city guards had witnessed his fit of madness, and no citizens pursued him. He tethered the horse again and pulled off his cloak, wadding it into a ball as he retraced his path to the marketplace.

A concerned crowd had gathered around Leonie, commiserating with her.

"It shouldn't be legal to drink so early in the day," one woman said as she gathered broken pottery shards into a pile. "These drunkards don't care for anyone's safety, including their own."

"You poor dear," said another. "Where's your husband to help you?"

Thorben shrank back into a sheltered nook along the wall. Leonie, voice thick with unshed tears, said, "He's not with me today."

"Shame on him. None of this is salvageable, child. You might as well go home and share the unfortunate news."

She sniffled but didn't leave, instead gathering broken shards into the bed of the handcart. Several others joined her, cleaning up the shattered pottery. With ever-increasing guilt, Thorben skirted back the way he had come, to a midpoint where he could watch for Alois and Leonie both.

Soon, she crossed his periphery, pulling the trash-laden cart behind her.

Conscious that he should be home before she arrived, he ran along a parallel road. He slipped into the hovel as she turned up the street. Huffing, he tried to calm himself. Should he exit again, help her drag the cart of spoiled goods back the rest of the way? But would she ask why he was so out of breath and sweating? Had she seen him shut the door?

"You coward," he uttered to himself. "Help that poor woman instead of creating more trouble for her."

He flung open the door but halted not two steps past its threshold. Leonie had already arrived, sidling the handcart up to the front aspect of the hut. Their eyes met, and her stoic expression cracked.

She dropped the cart handles and threw herself into his arms, bursting into tears. Thorben, in his astonishment, tucked her close and held her tight. They stood together for a long moment. Every sob that shook her frame condemned him.

He had done this, had driven this poor girl to a breaking point. Why had he followed that rash idea? Was he truly so frightened of Alois finding him?

But it wasn't Alois he feared; it was Leonie herself, the revulsion that would sweep upon her when she finally learned the truth of who he was. In destroying her pottery stall, he hadn't acted for her safety, as he'd originally told himself. He'd acted for his own, to prevent Alois from seeing and identifying him to her.

Alois, who might even now be prowling the streets in search of the lovely princess.

"Come inside," Thorben whispered as her tears subsided into hiccups. Carefully he ushered her into the hovel. He could tend to the cart full of broken pottery later, but getting Leonie herself off the street took precedence.

Within their single room, she despondently pulled the wimple from her head and cast it aside, her pale hair tumbling around her. With shuddering breath, she said, "Everything's ruined. I set up near the corner of the market, and a drunk horseman trampled through it all."

No mention of the Prince of Arbenia. The first time she had sold pottery, she had been so apprehensive of someone she knew recognizing her. Now it wasn't worth disclosing?

He swallowed, confused. "Why did you not set up in the same spot as before? Surely no one else took that tiny space between the farmer and the spice merchant."

She flinched, not quite meeting his gaze. "I thought it best . . . not to sit where I would have the same customers again. People don't buy new pottery every week, do they?"

"Probably not," he allowed, his conscience twinging like a badly stubbed toe.

"And now it's all destroyed, and it's my fault—!" Her voice hitched high on these final words, her tears surging anew.

"Oh, no no." He swooped in and gathered her again. "None of this is your fault, absolutely none of it. It's my fault. I should've been with you."

She shook her head, face buried against his chest and fingers curled into his shirt. "What am I supposed to do? What am I supposed to do when you're gone?"

His whole body froze, his breath suddenly shallow. The princess, sensing this shift, lifted red-rimmed eyes to meet his gaze.

How could she be so beautiful even when distraught?

"Leonie, you don't want to stay married to me," he said in a hollow voice. "You don't want to be married at all, remember?"

Her tears built again, sparkling as they tumbled down her cheeks. "I didn't want to leave Felstark Castle. I can't go back there, and I can't stay here, and I have no way of moving forward, because I ruin everything I try to do on my own."

He stooped, grasping her shoulders, pinning her with a stern stare. "*You* did not ruin this. You were brilliant. Just because some fool on a horse crashed through your wares doesn't make you any less capable of selling them."

"I don't want to go back to the market, Tor!"

"No, of course not." He tugged her again into his arms, holding her tight, wishing he were not such a coward. Confessing now was impossible, though. She would turn from despair to fury. Although he deserved every epithet she might hurl at him, he could not bear it.

This maddening, enchanting woman! Why could she not stay sarcastic and superior so that he could maintain his indifference? Instead of keeping her at arm's length as he'd planned, he was stroking her hair and whispering reassurances in her ears.

"You don't have to go back to the market. Where would you like to go?"

She gripped his shirt, staring at his chest. Hesitantly she said, "I could travel with you." The eyes that flitted up to meet his held such timid hope that he inwardly cursed.

Never in his life had he been so sorely tempted—and so completely condemned.

She read a denial in his dismay and rested her forehead against him again, her breath uneven.

Haltingly he said, "You don't want to travel with me. You already know I'm a horrible companion."

A watery chuckle bubbled from her, and she stepped decisively away. As she wiped tears with her wrist, she nodded. "That's true. What a foolish suggestion." Cynicism tainted her humor.

"It wasn't foolish," Thorben murmured. "I'm just no match for you."

Much as he dearly wished otherwise.

The comment elicited another wry laugh. "I have no match. Every eligible nobleman across the Twelve Kingdoms once pursued me, and the beggar who won me never wanted me in the first place."

At least one of those noblemen still pursued her. Did she not think that worth examination? But Thorben, who was not supposed to know of Alois's appearance, could not bring it up. He could only answer the accusation laid at his door. "It's not a matter of want. I don't deserve you."

Her head snapped up, a spark kindling in her blue eyes. "So you do want me, then?"

Inwardly he panicked. "That's irrelevant."

Why had he not simply denied it? She brightened, fragments of hope building in her to his utter dismay. "It's completely relevant to me. If it's true, you're being stubborn for no reason at all."

"*You're* being stubborn," he said, like a child caught in an argument he couldn't win. "Whoever heard of a princess settling for a beggar?"

She flung her arms outward, emphasizing their humble domain. "I'm not a princess anymore. I've been disowned. And if I were, whoever heard of a beggar denying a princess what she wants?"

"You don't know what you want!"

Leonie's mouth flattened. Thorben had just enough time to second-guess his rash accusation before she swept forward and cupped his face in both hands. Her sudden kiss, delivered on tiptoe, shot a wave of euphoria through him.

How had it come to this? Two camps warred within him: the yearning that leapt toward her and the guilt that demanded he retreat.

Guilt won, though not before yearning revealed too much. He broke off the embrace on a backward step, pushing against her shoulders to restore space between them. "You don't understand. There are things you don't know—"

"I don't need to know everything," she said. "Neither of us needs to know everything."

He shook his head. "You're only choosing this because you see no other option."

Something akin to hurt crossed her face. She stepped backward as well. "And you're only rejecting it because you have other choices you can make."

Her hopeless accusation snapped his self-restraint. On a rumbled growl, he swept her into his arms and kissed her with abandon, every repressed desire finding harbor in her willing lips, in the hands that rose to encircle his neck, in the body that crushed against his.

It was a mistake, but an exhilarating one.

"Do not misunderstand," he said, voice low and ragged. "I don't reject this because I have other choices. It's a matter of honor."

"We are married. Where's your honor toward that?"

"You know that ceremony was a sham, Leonie."

This near, she was positively intoxicating. "It doesn't have to be."

Curse him, but he wished that were true. "Yes, it does," he said, releasing her and stepping decisively away. He shook his head, waving her off. "I can't think straight when I'm with you. I'm going to dispose of your broken pottery."

And perhaps take a cold swim in the river, and maybe slam his head against a brick wall. He fled the house before she could protest or demand to come along. In the moment, he didn't trust himself to deny her anything less than his whole and ardent devotion, and that only because of the crown she'd already said she despised.

Briefly he imagined becoming Tor the beggar in earnest, a poor and mediocre traveling minstrel. Bert could ascend to the throne of Hauke on his majority, and everyone could forget Thorben, the king-who-wasn't.

It would never work; first, because he could never escape his family, and second, because Leonie deserved better than a wretched deceiver as her life's partner.

"Tor, you mealy coward," he uttered under his breath.

CHAPTER 12

He almost didn't return to the hovel that night. When he finally approached, part of him hoped that Leonie had left.

No such luck. Instead, a savory scent embraced him on the threshold. The princess looked up from the hearth, a picture of domestic beauty as she stirred the pot over the fire. For an instant she tensed, her grip tightening on the ladle.

"I'm sorry about earlier," Thorben gruffly said.

Her posture relaxed. "About kissing me, or about leaving?"

"Both."

She nodded and returned her attention to the simmering pot.

He breathed deep and plunged ahead. "If you knew the truth—when you learn it—you'll hate me."

"Do you have another wife?" she flatly asked.

"What? No."

A low, breathy laugh escaped her. It occurred to him that she already knew as much and was needling him. Eager to move past the tangled emotions of the day, he asked, "What are you cooking?"

"A woman from the market brought us some vegetables and a bit of beef as consolation for the broken dishes. I didn't realize anyone knew where we lived."

She seemed torn between gratitude and worry. Thorben, too, found this detail concerning. Of course the young couple had been in the area long enough for other residents to observe their comings and goings, but he hadn't really believed anyone was paying attention.

"I thought you didn't know how to cook."

"I don't. She helped me chop everything and toss it in the pot with some water, then said to let it boil until evening. It might be the worst thing we've ever eaten." She offered him a faint, upturned smile and returned to stirring.

He dug his fingernails into his palms, fighting the urge to join her at the hearth. "I'm sure it will taste fine."

Her nose wrinkled. She leaned forward to sniff the pot and said, "I don't know. She threw some leaves in as well and said I had to fish them out before we eat. I'm not sure I can find them again."

He laughed despite himself. At the hearth, Leonie suppressed a smile, maintaining her tranquility as she stirred.

This was pure torture. He needed to speak, to confess and accept the revulsion that would result. He inhaled, steeled himself against impending derision, and—

A percussive knock shook the door behind him. Thorben whirled, confused, and Leonie rose from the hearthstones, ladle still in hand.

"Tor, are you in there?" called a familiar voice.

His heart lurched. He yanked the door open to find Marco on the tiny front step. The advisor looked grim. He ducked into the hovel, his gaze briefly flitting past his king before returning.

"Who is this?" Leonie lightly asked, twisting the ladle as she came to stand beside Thorben.

His confusion magnified. Marco had been next to him at the party in Felstark, but perhaps she hadn't noticed him in her haste to insult. "He's my contact at the castle," he said, with a fleeting, pleading glance to his advisor.

Marco dipped his head, bowing to Leonie. His greeting sent a chill down Thorben's spine. "Your Highness, it's good to see you again."

The princess stiffened. With a splinter of ice in her voice, she asked. "Have we met?"

"No, not officially. We have been in the same room before, however." He shifted back to his tattered king. "Everything's gone sour. Alois of Arbenia showed up at the castle this afternoon. He brought a tale of an Elisian princess married to a beggar, and the king's council has connected that with *your* unique circumstances."

Thorben uttered an oath under his breath.

"Does that mean they won't approve the annulment?" Leonie innocently asked.

He shot her a warning glance. Marco, oblivious, said, "It means they have to consider political implications beyond offending King Eustis, Your Highness. It's one thing to dissolve a marriage between two non-consenting parties and quite another when one of those parties is a foreign princess. And I'm in disgrace for not disclosing your identity from the start, of course."

Her brows arched. "Did you know my identity?"

"I didn't tell him," Thorben said before Marco could answer.

"Ah," she said and twisted the ladle again.

He bristled. "It shouldn't matter, our rank. A forced marriage shouldn't stand just because someone has too much status, or not enough."

"You thought it would lessen our chances for an annulment if they knew," she said, and the laugh that followed held little mirth. "You must be desperate to be rid of me."

"Leonie—"

"Is this the truth that's supposed to make me hate you? I think it's hilarious. Serves you right if we get stuck together." So saying, she returned to the hearth and her simmering stew.

Behind her back Marco silently tipped his head toward the street, portent of more news to share.

"I'll be back shortly," Thorben said over his shoulder.

"Fine. This should be ready soon. Your *contact* is welcome to stay if he wants to try a beggar woman's first attempt at cooking."

He grunted and shut the door behind him, cutting off the warmth of the hearth and the princess who tended it. Before Marco could speak a word, he tugged him in the direction of the river.

"No tavern tonight?" his advisor wryly asked.

"Tell me the worst," Thorben said.

"Your mother suspects."

He swore and increased his pace. "How?"

"Because you were supposed to be with Alois, who has told her that you parted ways in Felstark the day after the party. I'm in disgrace for that as well. I had to tell her you took guards from the embassy with you after ordering me and Bert to go home, and that I don't know where you ended up if not with Alois. She's sending a search party into Elisia. She wants Leonie found and brought to the castle, too."

Thorben stopped short, thunderstruck. "She can't! Leonie doesn't want to go there!"

"She did seem rather pleased that the annulment might fail," said Marco with a backward glance to the hovel and the princess hidden within.

The evening shadows hid Thorben's rising blush. "That's only because she thinks I'm a beggar. A pox on Alois and his meddling! I should have trampled him with his own horse this morning."

"Then you knew he was here?"

Reluctantly he nodded. "He saw Leonie in the market. She called him a dullard again, and he decided she needed rescuing from her wretched husband—whom he did *not* see, I might add."

A frown wrinkled Marco's brow. "So how did he end up at the castle?"

Thorben sighed as though the weight of a thousand stones lay upon his shoulders. They resumed their walk, and the morning's events tumbled from him in a halting confession.

"So she doesn't know that *you* rode the horse that plowed through her stall?" Marco asked when the narrative ended.

"And she didn't even mention Alois. She seemed far more upset about broken dishes than about the man who was plotting to kidnap her."

The advisor puffed his cheeks on a heavy exhale. "To be fair, she didn't know about his plot. Almost getting trampled was probably her greater concern. He's still looking for her, you know. That's part of the reason your mother wants her at the castle."

Thorben scowled. "What do you mean?"

"Queen Julika declined housing Alois for the night, thanks to your absence, but suggested that he stay with me instead." He shot a mirthless smile to his king, nicely communicating his enthusiasm for this honor. "My father gave him a room, and Alois has expressed his intention to stay in Swifthaven until he finds Leonie again."

"Why would my mother want her at the castle, then?"

"Because she doesn't want to add Arbenia into this political mess. Alois might frame himself as a rescuing hero, but he comes across as obsessive. It's bad enough that we might have to nullify King Eustis's own daughter's marriage, but if we also have to admit we allowed a foreign prince to carry her off . . ."

A fragment of hope crystalized within Thorben. "So there's still a chance the annulment could happen?"

Marco chuckled, as though enjoying a private joke. "Oh, yes."

Thorben, increasingly cagey, prompted him. "But . . . ?"

"Well, it has to be Leonie's choice, doesn't it? Our council won't dissolve a foreign princess's marriage if the princess herself doesn't object to it."

He stopped walking again, overcome with dismay. "That is quite possibly the worst thing you could have told me." He raked both hands through his hair and looked skyward, to the twinkling stars.

"She doesn't want it annulled?" Marco guessed.

"She doesn't know what she wants!"

This argument was no more convincing to Marco than it had been to Leonie earlier in the day. The advisor scowled. "Tell her who you are, you fool."

"And then what? We both return to the castle, where my mother will insist on housing her until the annulment can be finalized? And then? Do we send her back to her father? Or onward to Arbenia?"

"You're assuming she'll reject you as king."

"I'm not *assuming*. She has flat told me that she doesn't want to be the Queen of Hauke or anywhere else. If I want this annulment, the *easiest* way to get it would be to tell her who I am!"

Marco stepped back a pace, one brow arching. "*If* you want it . . . ?"

Thorben silently cursed his slip of the tongue. "Not *if*. I do want it, but I want it as Tor the beggar, where I can exit with my dignity intact. If I receive it as Thorben of Hauke—or as *King Thrushbeard*, as Alois is still calling me—I will be the laughingstock of the Twelve Kingdoms."

"That's quite the dilemma," Marco mused, with not an ounce of sympathy in his voice.

His king spared him a withering glance and returned to the problem at hand. "Can't you tell my mother that you've found Leonie but she doesn't wish to come to the castle?"

"I don't think she'll accept that. She wants to know that Leonie's provided for."

"Then what about a castle job? Can we send her on the pretense that she's working there? My mother will know that she's receiving proper wages, and Leonie can maintain this beggar status she seems to enjoy."

"Will Leonie accept a job there?" Marco asked.

Thorben's breath left him in a whoosh. "I don't know. She makes no sense! Why would she want a mere beggar when she has scorned dukes and earls and princes?"

"And at least one king," said Marco mildly.

The comment earned him a dry glance. Thorben shook his head. "There's something going on with her, some underlying fear or misconception that must drive this strange aversion to nobility."

What had she said earlier? A remark he had hardly noticed at the time: "Neither of us needs to know everything." Some specter haunted Leonie in the same way that Thorben's true identity haunted him. Fragments of evidence had surfaced during the past week, and he had ignored them because he was too absorbed in his own troubles.

"Tor, have you considered that she already knows who you are?" Marco abruptly asked. When his king looked sharply to him, he huffed a laugh. "The beard makes you look different, but not *that* different. You're still obviously Thorben of Hauke to anyone who knows you."

Could that be it? Was Leonie torturing him on purpose? All those comments about Hauke and King Thrushbeard, had she made them as a dig at the very man beside her?

Had she kissed him today knowing he was a king instead of a beggar?

It couldn't be. "She only saw me once, and only long enough to insult me. I genuinely believe she doesn't know."

"Then perhaps she believes her father's unkindness is universal for those in power."

"That's idiotic. She's too intelligent to think that."

The advisor shrugged. "Trauma does strange things to people. Short of asking her directly, you're not likely to figure it out. So, what are you going to do?"

Whatever mystery nested in the princess's soul, she would not easily disclose it. She had been too ready to dismiss his secrets rather than trade for information about herself.

"Let's tell her the queen wants her brought to the castle. If she balks, which I'm certain she will, we can propose the compromise of a job there."

"And what if your mother balks at that compromise?"

"Remind her that Leonie is a foreign princess, free to make her own decisions."

Marco nodded, but he voiced one other possibility. "What if she does go to the castle, and between her account and your mother's, she learns your true identity?"

"So be it," said Thorben with a heavy sigh. "I'd almost prefer someone else tell her so that I never have to."

"I can, if you'd like."

"You can go to the devil, too."

Laughter shook his advisor's frame.

Their path turned away from the river, back the direction they had come. The savory aroma greeted them at the hovel's door. Leonie promptly began dishing stew into bowls from a stack of three beside her. She extended the first to Marco. "You're staying, I assume?"

He received it with a murmured, "For a bit. Thank you, Your Highness."

"No titles. I'm just Leonie here." She ladled Thorben's portion and offered it to him.

"Did you find the leaves again?" he wryly asked, peering into the cloudy broth. She half-shrugged, mischief on her face. He sipped from the edge of the bowl but found nothing wrong with the meal, aside from a general lack of flavor.

Leonie, sampling her own, wrinkled her nose. "It's missing something."

"It's delicious," Marco assured her.

She wagged dismissive fingers at him. "You would say that regardless. Tor, you don't mince words to spare my feelings. What's wrong with it?"

"No salt," he said, and he sipped again. "It's too expensive for beggars to keep on hand, but you would be accustomed to it in castle food."

Her brows arched and she tasted her stew again. "I think you're right. I suppose I should get used to bland food."

"There's no reason you have to." This remark earned him a scowl. He cleared his throat and pressed ahead. "Now that Queen Julika knows you're in Hauke, she wants you brought to the castle."

Leonie froze, suddenly looking like she was made of glass. Quietly she said, "She can't make me. I'm not one of her citizens."

"But I am," Thorben said. "And we both have experience with a monarch forcing his will on those who don't want it."

"Is Queen Julika like that?"

He deferred this question to Marco, who shifted uncomfortably. "She would never force anyone to marry, like your father did. She does have a domineering reputation, though. We thought maybe she—and you—would accept a compromise."

The princess glanced between them suspiciously. "What compromise?"

"A job. Tor says you've been looking for a way to earn money. If you're working at the castle, the queen will know your needs are being met, which is her primary concern."

Her expression twisted. "I don't want to work at the castle. I don't want to go within three miles of it!"

"Technically, you're already within two," said Marco. Thorben jostled him. "That is, there's nothing scary about Swifthaven Castle. The servants receive excellent wages, and they're treated with respect. You'd command more authority as a guest of the queen than as a worker, but we think she'd allow the latter arrangement."

Leonie shifted pleading eyes to Thorben. "Can't we just leave? You want to travel. I won't be a burden on you, I swear—!"

He shook his head. "No. Even if we could, we'd have a hundred Haukien soldiers chasing after us. I think you should try the job."

"But there will be a uniform, and I don't have that."

"The castle provides it," said Marco, frowning—and with good reason. Felstark Castle would have provided their servants' uniforms as well. Leonie, who used to be surrounded with attendants, should have known that.

She tried a different avenue of protest. "I don't know anyone there, and there must be a hundred people—!" Her voice cut out on a fluttering breath.

Thorben, suspicious, straightened his spine a fraction more. "Are you afraid of crowds?"

"Of course I'm not," she snapped, a blush rising on her cheeks. "How could I have braved the marketplace so many times if I were?"

She'd clung to him on their first trek through that area, but on pretense that she didn't want to get lost. Something about his accusation had struck too close to the mark, though. He inwardly searched for clues.

A small growl rumbled in Leonie's throat. "If you're so desperate for me to work there, I'll do it. I won't like it, but I'll do it. And where will you be?"

Thorben grunted. "Holing up here, probably. It seems this Alois of Arbenia who reported you also wants to do me bodily harm."

"I won't go to the castle if *he's* there," said Leonie, bristling.

Marco intervened before she could change her mind about their compromise. "He's not at the castle. He's still in the city but staying with my father. I think he intends to remain until he can find and rescue you."

"More than a dullard," she muttered. "Why do some men never accept 'no' for an answer?"

Thorben, sensing an angle they could leverage, said, "You're safer at the castle than here on the streets. He can spend his days searching for you while you're blending in with a whole crew of servants."

She grimaced but raised no objection.

Marco departed shortly thereafter to carry this proposal to the queen. Thorben could only hope that his mother accepted it. More likely, she would pin down the king's advisor and force the whole truth from him, and they'd have a platoon of guards at the hovel door by midnight.

At this point, it hardly mattered. He should confess himself and accept the inevitable rejection.

CHAPTER 13

No guards appeared overnight, but Marco was on their doorstep again shortly after dawn, bearing a parcel wrapped in brown paper. "A castle uniform," he said as he solemnly handed this item to Leonie.

Thorben stepped outside with his advisor and shut the door, giving her the privacy to change. His voice lowered to a whisper. "Our illustrious queen accepted the proposal, then?"

"She doesn't like it, but you were right. She won't interfere too much with the whims of a foreign princess. How much longer for this charade, Tor? Your coronation is in ten days."

He made a shushing noise, conscious that Leonie might try to eavesdrop. "Get Alois out of the kingdom first. I don't want him skulking around."

"I thought your fondest wish was for Leonie to accept his suit and go with him," Marco dryly said. When he received a dour glare for this comment, he chuckled. "You're properly whipped, aren't you."

It wasn't a question. They both knew the state of the young king's heart.

Leonie appeared minutes later, clad in the gray dress worn by maids and kitchen helpers in Swifthaven Castle. She peered first at Thorben and then at Marco, a wrinkle between her brows. "I look like a nun."

"Hardly," Thorben said. "Your cap is nothing close to a wimple."

Indeed, the snowy white cap allowed her pale hair to flow down her back, making her easily identifiable in a crowd of similarly dressed servants. She sniffed, unimpressed with the difference, and glanced up the street in the direction of the castle.

"Having second thoughts?" Marco asked.

Thorben elbowed him, but Leonie merely grumbled, "A pox on Queen Julika of Hauke. Is she going to summon me for an interrogation while I'm there?"

"I believe she intends to give you your space," said Marco.

"And what of her children? Do they know I'm coming?"

"Not that I'm aware."

"Not even Thrushbeard?" Leonie sharply said.

Marco and Thorben exchanged a glance. "He's still abroad," said the advisor.

"Good. I don't want his attention any more than I want the dullard's."

Thorben, before he could stop himself, sarcastically asked, "Did he court you as well?"

Leonie had the grace to blush and avert her gaze. "No, but he appeared at the choosing, which is bad enough."

"He didn't really have a choice in that," Marco said. At her frown, and likely realizing his remark could be construed as a slight, he hastened to clarify. "Not to diminish Your Highness's natural allure, but our queen wouldn't let him out of the castle unless he promised to make an appearance in Felstark. Now he's off on a last lark before he officially ascends the throne."

Tonelessly she said, "How lucky for him."

Marco chortled. "That's debatable. His mother's going to have his hide when he turns up again."

Thorben suppressed a shiver, doing everything in his power to pretend he couldn't care less about the King of Hauke's personal problems. Queen Julika embodied kindness and hospitality when people did as she expected. When difficulties arose, though, she became so deathly reserved that her own attendants couldn't bow and scrape out of the room fast enough.

Leonie truly was indifferent. "As long as she doesn't plan to annul one marriage and force me into another, I don't care."

"She can't force her son to marry," Thorben said, annoyance loosening his tongue. "Haukien law forbids it. No one can force the king to take a bride he doesn't want."

"Well," Marco hedged, half-grinning, but Thorben shot him such an acidic glare that he swallowed his bubbling mirth. Instead, he shrugged. "She did strong-arm him to Felstark. Presumably he would've accepted an alliance there had one been offered, but there would've at least been a façade of choice."

"I never would have chosen him," Leonie said darkly.

"Yes, he was banking on that," the king's advisor replied. "Again, no insult to your charms, Your Highness."

She huffed and tapped her toes on the cobblestones. "Should we go? I don't suppose dawdling here will change the queen's mind."

Thorben, who had heard quite enough chatter against himself, gestured up the road. "No, it won't. I hope you have a nice time."

Dismay crossed her face. "You're not walking there with me?"

"I have no business at the castle."

"Except that *your wife* is starting to work there today."

Tempted though he was to quip something about a wife he never would have chosen, he simply shrugged. "What can I say? I'm a horrible husband. Tell them you want an annulment and be rid of me."

Leonie clenched her jaw, nostrils flaring.

He pushed the issue. "They'll listen to you sooner than they will a mere beggar."

She leaned close and hissed, "Maybe I'll tell them to cancel the annulment instead."

A sarcastic laugh escaped him. "You'll dearly regret it if you do."

"Your Highness, please," Marco interjected, shifting from one foot to the other as he observed the pair. "If we delay too long, Queen Julika might assume you left the city during the night. She will send soldiers."

Leonie ignored this concern to ask Thorben, "Are you really going to leave me in the hands of someone I don't even know?"

He shrugged. "I'm sure he's trustworthy. His father's a duke."

On a low growl, she wrapped around his elbow and jerked him into the road. He stumbled for two steps before getting his feet under him. Leonie, seething, kept her attention forward, walking as though she had a willing escort instead of a grudging one.

Thorben suppressed a grin and submitted instead of pulling away. The nearer they got to the castle, the more likely it was for someone to recognize him, but not this early in the day. Most of the noble class wouldn't be at their breakfast table before noon, let alone out on the street.

Alois certainly never rose with the sun, so he had no worries from that quarter.

As they neared the castle, as its towers loomed and the city became finer and grander, an odd nostalgia lodged in Thorben's chest. He'd been living in the slums of Swifthaven for only a week, but it seemed like a lifetime.

Unlike in Felstark, parklands surrounded the castle here, the better to allow full view of the kingdom's most illustrious residence. Birds chirped in the stately trees that lined walkways and shaded benches. Later in the day, nobles and gentry would promenade through the lovely scenery, but all was calm now.

What would Leonie do if he strode with her past the guards and resumed his proper place? She was bound to hear his real name spoken while at work, without the lisping consonant that her people always used when addressing him. Would she connect Tor with Thorben? Would she assume it was a common name in Hauke?

If he still held her in contempt, now would be the perfect moment for revenge. Instead, he wanted to hold the connection between them as long as possible before it collapsed.

His steps slowed when the castle gates came into view, until he stopped. Leonie, pausing, glanced up at him.

"This is as far as I go. I think you'll be safe enough for the next hundred yards."

She didn't immediately release his arm. "Will you be here tonight, to walk me home?"

"And risk the Prince of Arbenia mangling me?"

Her scowl renewed. "He doesn't know what you look like."

Behind him, Marco suppressed a chortle. Thorben, ignoring this, said, "But he'll draw conclusions if he sees you and me together."

She glanced around herself. "I don't know that I can find my way home."

"The nights are warm. You could sleep in an alley." His breath left him when she thrust an elbow into his ribcage. On a breathy laugh he doubled over. He couldn't resist another tease. "Ask for a bed at the castle, then. I'm sure they'll give it to you."

A hint of despair flashed across her face. "Stop talking like you're abandoning me. Please, just come at the end of the day. I'm sure the dullard has better things to do than patrol the streets at dinnertime. I'm sure you could best him in a fight, too. If his fists are on par with his wits, you'll lay him flat with a single punch."

"What makes you think I know how to punch anyone, or that I'd want to?" Thorben asked.

Leonie, considering this question, said, "I thought all beggars knew how to fight."

"Public brawling is not something we encourage in Swifthaven," said Marco, stepping into the conversation before it could further devolve. "I'll make certain that Alois is sitting down to a long and opulent meal at sunset, Your Highness, so as to avoid any altercations when your husband comes for you." He shifted a telling look to his king, who grimaced and looked to Leonie.

Her hopeful, pleading eyes would have dropped a weaker man to his knees. Only a heart of stone could deny her request.

"I'll be here at sunset," he grudgingly said.

He spent his day walking the lower wards of the city, floppy-brimmed hat drooping over his forehead. Although it was interesting to tread unknown among his subjects, he felt oddly alone.

Ridiculous. He'd spent enough time away from Leonie since their arrival in Hauke. She hadn't become an ever-present fixture in his life.

Their time left together was dwindling, though. Where would she go after she learned the truth? To Arbenia or one of the other Twelve Kingdoms? She certainly wouldn't continue as a servant in his castle, nor did he want her to. Whatever strange notion had resigned her to the life of a beggar, she lacked the skills and temperament to remain one.

As the sun descended toward the horizon, he retraced his steps to their chosen meeting place, keeping his hat low and his gaze downcast. Too many carriages on the road made him skittish. By the time he arrived near the castle gates, although the parklands were mostly deserted, he half-expected some well-meaning noble to shout his name.

Perhaps Leonie wouldn't emerge. Perhaps she'd deduced the truth while at work in his kitchens.

He almost wished it were so.

And yet, when the last rays of the dying sun illuminated her pale hair and smiling face, his heart flip-flopped and relief flooded through him. He pulled off his hat and, twisting it in his hands, rose from the bench where he'd been waiting.

She skipped through the gates but paused a dozen yards beyond them, crestfallen as she looked up and down the street and into the parklands. Her gaze flitted right past him.

"Leonie!" he called, and waved his hat. "Over here!"

She started, for an instant apprehensive. That tension drained as quickly as it appeared, and she dashed straight for him. Before he could speak another word, she collided into him, wrapping her arms around him and burying her face in his chest.

His pulse spiked when she breathed deep against him.

"This is more of a greeting than I expected," he said.

She beamed up at him. "You came. The least I can do is reward you."

"What makes you think it's a reward?"

Her expression contorted. She shifted to his side, somehow weaseling herself under his arm as she kept one of hers around his waist. In this position, his hand draped over her shoulder. Before he could retract it, she grasped it with her free hand.

A passerby might have mistaken them for a loving couple instead of a pair of hapless fools.

"I brought you dinner," she said as they started the walk home, a note of triumph in her voice.

"Something you made?"

"No, I scrubbed pots all day. I'll have washer-woman hands in no time, like a proper beggar's wife should."

"That won't suit you," Thorben said.

She flashed him a scowl. "It'll have to, since that's what I am now." Then she schooled away her annoyance in favor of good cheer. "Anyway, all the servants divided up the leftovers from the day's meals, and I got my fair share, plus extra for you. Cook insisted."

"Where did you put it?" he asked, noting her free hands.

"Here. They gave me a pocket to wear, and it's deep enough to hold a couple of earthenware jars."

He glanced down to her slim waist. Tied alongside the servant's apron, she wore an external pocket, its fabric the same hue as her dress, with darker embroidery along its edges. "It's a very fine pocket."

"All the women wear them. The men have pockets sown into their trousers, I suppose. I don't care."

He suppressed a laugh. "You sound like you had a good time."

A furrow cut between her brows, the face she always made when she was considering something. "I wouldn't say it was a *good* time, but it wasn't as awful as I expected. They all call me 'Blondie,' and no one requires me to remember their names. Most of them didn't even tell me what they were, because they call each other by nicknames or positions anyway."

Thorben peered down at her in the falling gloom, a suspicion brushing against his thoughts. "Do you have trouble remembering names?"

Leonie stiffened beneath his arm. "No, of course not. But if I'm getting thrown in with hundreds of servants, there are too many to learn all at once."

"At least a dozen of them are called Hetty or Hans, I'm sure."

Her footsteps slowed as she pondered this. "I think I might have met two different Hettys today."

"You *think?*"

She batted the question aside. "Maybe I heard wrong. It doesn't matter. I'll probably meet another half-dozen tomorrow."

"Then you're returning?"

"If the queen demands it, do I have a choice?"

He conceded this point, though he thought she'd be less eager to serve in a castle she'd sneered at reigning over.

At some point during their walk home, she interlaced her fingers with his and more comfortably tucked herself at his side. Thorben considered withdrawing, but her words from that morning played upon his mind. She still held the King of Hauke in contempt. In a way, it assuaged his ruffled feelings for her to show him such affection without knowing his true identity.

Pathetically, he enjoyed the simple contact.

Night had fully fallen by the time they entered their dark hovel. He nursed their banked coals into a fire as Leonie removed their dinner from her pocket and meted portions for each of them. She joined him in companionable silence in front of the hearth and handed him his plate.

The first bite—savory roast beef in gravy—melted in his mouth, providing reason enough to abandon this ridiculous charade. He was speechless for so long that Leonie broke into an impish laugh.

"You look like you've never tasted proper food before!"

He swallowed another delectable morsel. "The castle has resources that beggars can't afford. Only a fool would choose this life over one that allowed such luxury every day."

Her smile faltered. "The servants always take home leftovers. We can have this luxury every day from now on."

"Even after King Thrushbeard returns?"

A brittleness descended upon her. She regarded him for a long, silent moment, so solemn that his heart sank.

"We can't go on like this forever, Leonie," he softly said.

"He's off on a lark. He might not even notice me among the servants when he returns."

"You're a tulip in a field of wildflowers. You can't help but draw attention. Besides, wouldn't his mother tell him you're there?"

She waved him off with dismissive fingers, though her expression had shuttered. "Your castle contact said Thrushbeard didn't want anything to do with me. I'm married now. There's no reason to suspect he'll disregard that like the dullard from Arbenia does."

"He's more likely to support the annulment and ship you from the kingdom," Thorben said.

Leonie stiffened. "Why would you think that?"

He shrugged. "If he didn't want his own marriage arranged, he wouldn't approve of a forced marriage for anyone else. The king's council certainly believed that was his view: before they knew who you were, they were only waiting for his return to end things."

She ducked her head to catch his gaze. The low light of the fire gleamed off sudden tears in her eyes. "Why are you *so* eager to be rid of me?"

The anguish in that question wrung his heart. He caught her hand on instinct, holding tight so that she couldn't withdraw. "Why are *you* so eager to stay? It can't last. We both know it can't. The sooner we accept that, the less pain we'll have when this is finally over."

"I hate you," she said, voice thick with tears, but she squeezed his hand instead of pulling from him.

Ruefully, Thorben said, "Again, why are you so eager to stay?"

"Because I *like* you. And you like me too, if you're honest enough to admit it."

A grim laugh cut from his throat. "I can't imagine why any sane man would like such an irrational creature. In one breath you hate me, and in the next you like me? We've known each other for barely more than a week, and much of that under duress. How will you feel six months from now, when your hands have grown calluses, and snow and ice block your path to the castle, and we have hardly enough fuel each day to keep the bitter winds out of the cracks and crevices of this miserable hut? How will you feel when you discover sides of me you can't fathom in such a shallow acquaintance? Annul the marriage, Leonie. There are better prospects for you than to play servant in a foreign king's household and come home to a beggar husband you never would have chosen."

She listened to this speech with growing solemnity, but when it ended, even as unshed tears shimmered in her eyes, she raised his hand to her lips and fiercely kissed his knuckles. "It's that heartless logic that I hate, and it's that same heartless logic that tells me to stay. If you've thought that far ahead, you can think of solutions to every problem you've listed. And *don't* tell me annulment is the only way. If you really wanted to leave me, you'd have done it already."

He shook his head but conceded the point. "Fair enough." A wry smile pulled one corner of his mouth. "Maybe the queen will give me a title to restore your good graces."

Leonie's brows arched. "Wouldn't Thrushbeard have to award it?"

He'd meant the remark as a joke. Why did she seem to be considering it? More importantly, why did that prospect not repulse her? He frowned. "I thought you hated nobles."

She frowned right back. "Why should I?"

"Because—" His voice cut out, his mind cascading backward in time. She'd certainly held every noble at her choosing party in contempt. But that wasn't quite right. She was on good terms with Ursinbau and his wife. The duke wasn't trying to marry her, though. So was it vitriol only for her suitors?

Not privy to his thoughts, she said, "I was born a princess. Why would you think I hate nobles?"

"Because you speak nothing but unkindness of them."

She shifted uncomfortably. "It's not *personal.* People born with titles are used to getting everything they want. You have to be firm if your wishes run counter to theirs, and even then they sometimes ignore you."

"But . . ." He sat up straight, letting go of her hand as he fumbled to understand. "If you don't mind being married to a beggar you've only just met, and you wouldn't mind that beggar receiving a title, why would you object to marrying a nobleman you've only just met who already has a title? You make no sense."

She bristled. "I don't have to make sense. Just because I didn't choose to marry you doesn't mean I can't accept the circumstance as a stroke of good fortune."

"But it was *bad* fortune, for both of us!"

Her mouth pressed into a firm line, her brows cinched tight. Thorben, conscious that he had trampled her feelings yet again, fell silent, waiting for her response.

After an interminable, awkward stretch of time, she finally pitched her voice light. "Men across the Twelve Kingdoms would consider marriage to me a stroke of incredible good luck."

"That's because they're only looking at your face and not considering your welfare."

A soft smile broke upon her, as on one newly enlightened. "Oh," she said on a quiet exhale, "I think I might love you after all."

The words, spoken so easily, melted every internal defense he'd established to keep her at arm's length. He shook his head, scrambling to restore them. "Leonie, no. Seeing you as a person instead of a trophy doesn't make me capable of meeting your needs—"

But she was already rising on her knees, wrapping her arms around his neck, enveloping him in a tight hug. Her hair and her clothes smelled of the castle soap, such a strange sense of *home* that he had not expected to assail him tonight.

He floundered to keep his senses intact. "We are not a match."

Her breath ghosted against his neck. "Don't worry. You don't have to love me back."

"Love has nothing to do with it," he stubbornly said. Against his better judgment, he slipped his arms around her, returning the embrace, drinking in her nearness while convincing himself that he could give her up when that moment arrived.

CHAPTER 14

Four more days passed, with a morning trek to Swifthaven Castle and an evening return to their hovel. Leonie recounted her work and pestered him with questions of how he'd spent their time apart. Sometimes they ambled down to the river to eat their dinner of leftovers by the glittering water. She didn't push him for signs of affection, but more often than not she caught his hand and swung their arms as they walked.

He let her, fully aware that he was digging his own grave the longer this charade continued.

Of Marco he saw nothing. The castle, with Leonie accounted for, seemed not to care about the beggar she went home with each night. He did see Alois several times, though from a distance. True to Marco's warning, the foreign prince was riding the streets of Swifthaven in search of his lost beloved. Thorben always ducked into an alley when he saw the telltale feather in Alois's cap bobbing above the crowds in the market or along the river walk.

Left to his own devices, the beggar king busked some days and merely observed on others. One afternoon he fished in the river with a borrowed pole and handed his catch off to a fishmonger.

The city was alive with preparations for his coronation only a week away. Pine boughs and garlands now festooned the streets as decorations, with extra attention along the route between the castle and the cathedral. Street vendors began selling commemorative favors: red ribbons, paper roses, and sugared pastries in the shape of a crown.

Had he occupied his proper place in the castle, he would have missed all of this. True, his mother was likely ready to strangle him, but that didn't diminish his enjoyment as he played spectator among his people. A king had only to go where his advisors told him on the designated day. His suit had been tailored months ago, and he'd memorized his part in the coronation already.

Yes, he was being irresponsible, but not *that* irresponsible. Or so he told himself.

On the evening of Leonie's fifth day as a kitchen maid, he strolled with confidence to his usual bench near the castle gates. No one in the upper class gave beggars a second glance, he'd learned, so he no longer worried about the passing carriages.

Tonight, though, a voice rang out across the park. "Tor!"

He froze in the act of sitting, eyes wide with horror. Over the grass, his brother Berthold ran, an enormous grin splitting his face. Thorben stood just in time to be clobbered with a hug.

Bert squeezed hard then held him at arm's length. "Ha! You look like trash!" In contrast, the young prince seemed as polished as a silver spoon, his expensive clothes a far cry from the tatters his older brother wore. "I'm on my way home from Ilsebeth's. Didn't think I'd see you here, this close to the castle walls. Mother will have your head if she spies you."

"She hasn't had the whole story from you already?" Thorben wryly asked.

Bert's chest puffed. "Hasn't even asked. She willingly believes that I, besotted with my lady love, returned home on purpose. I think you'll get the full brunt of her wrath, though. She's very tight-lipped when your name comes up."

An involuntary shiver ran down Thorben's spine. "Has her search party into Elisia returned?"

True to his carefree nature, Bert brushed aside the question. "Don't know a thing about it. I have been dutifully playing my role and spending my days elsewhere."

He'd been haunting Marco and Ilsebeth's house in other words. "I guess you see your share of Alois, then?" Thorben grimly asked.

Bert barked a laugh. "I'm taking notes on how to be an idiot in love. Ilsebeth says if she ever disappears into a foreign city, I'm to lodge with the first nobleman who offers me harbor, then eat him out of house and home while loudly proclaiming her perfections."

Comical as this portrayal was, Thorben frowned. "I thought he spent most of his time searching the streets for Leonie."

His brother huffed a derisive breath. "He goes out twice a day for an hour at a time and comes home in lamentations, absolutely famished. No one's bothered to tell him she's at the castle during his explorations, obviously."

"And no one better," Thorben darkly said. "Do you ever see her?"

Bert raised defensive hands, assuming an expression of utmost innocence. "I'm oblivious to any castle activities, especially where servants are concerned. Marco says Mother doesn't want any of us bothering Leonie. She thinks she'll get tired of cleaning up after lazy royals and reassert her title."

If only that were the case. A heavy sigh issued from Thorben. He doffed his hat to rake his fingers through his hair. "I somehow doubt that's how this ends."

"Regardless, I'm not supposed to know she's here—which works in my favor. I think we'd both rather she didn't recognize me as your fellow musician."

For an instant, Thorben had forgotten Bert's presence on that fateful night. He spared a self-conscious glance over his shoulder toward the gates. "Then you'd better scoot off. She meets me here when she finishes work."

"But wouldn't that be hilarious, her connecting the me from her party to the me from her wedding? I'd almost pay to see that recognition dawn."

Thorben, conscious of an itch to cuff his younger brother, forestalled only because a beggar could not lay hands on a prince. Within a stone's throw of the castle walls, guards could see them both and no doubt watched their every move. "It would *not* be hilarious," he said with tight control. "It would be disastrous. Go on, before she comes out."

Grinning, Bert clapped his brother on the back. He continued up the road to the gates, a spring in his step. Thorben donned his hat again, turning to watch his progress.

Within the gates Leonie appeared, and his heart stuttered. Ahead, Bert nearly tripped over his own two feet but caught himself. He shot his gaze upward, toward the top of the nearest guard tower, spine suddenly rigid as he kept walking.

It was like watching from afar as two carriages careened toward one another. Thorben dug his fingernails into his palms, waiting for the moment Leonie would glance at the young prince, for what reaction she would give.

Her eyes did flit toward him, but no sign of recognition followed. She continued without a hitch in her step, redirecting her gaze with no double take. Bert, as though oblivious to her presence, swaggered past, silently saluting the guards as he crossed into the castle grounds.

Confusion swept through Thorben. To be sure, she'd had little interaction with his brother. Bert had been behind him the night of their forced marriage, so she might not have seen him properly. She had openly bantered with him at her party, though, and he was dressed in that similar style now.

Across the distance, her eyes connected with Thorben's. For a split second she looked blank, and then a smile bloomed across her lovely face. She broke into a trot to meet him.

He remained rooted in place, mind reeling.

She always looked blank for that first split second when they met, and he had always dismissed it. *Why* had he always dismissed it?

When she joined him, she clasped his hands and announced, "I have roast goose tonight."

Thorben, hardly noticing the slim fingers curling around his own, said, "Did you see that man you just passed?"

Leonie glanced back over her shoulder, but Bert had already vanished beyond the gates. "What about him?"

"Did you recognize him?"

Her shoulders tensed and her smile faltered, but it renewed almost as quickly. "Should I have?"

His suspicions intensified. "That was Prince Berthold of Hauke, second in line for the throne."

Another backward glance. A dismissive shrug. "I've never met him before."

"Haven't you?" Thorben asked, his chest suddenly tight. He peered down at her, so intent that she stepped back a pace.

A faint, rueful laugh escaped her. "I don't know. Maybe I have. He didn't say anything when we passed, so he probably didn't recognize me either. The goose is still warm. We should hurry." She pulled him along, a quickness to her steps.

Thorben tripped along behind her, thoughts racing. She always pretended not to know Alois as well whenever they met.

Or, he'd assumed it was pretense.

His suspicions pushed past his lips. "Leonie, can you not recognize faces?"

Her steps hitched, and a too-high laugh emitted from her. "What are you on about? Of course I can." But her breath was suddenly shallow, and two spots of pink burned on her cheeks.

He strode in front of her and planted his hands on her shoulders, forcing her to stop. "What does your father look like?"

A wildness flitted through her eyes. "What is wrong with you? You met him once yourself. You know what he looks like."

"Humor me."

"Two eyes, a nose, and a mouth, just like most everyone else," she said sarcastically. Then she shrugged out from under his hold and continued walking. "I've had a long day, Tor. I just want to go home and eat."

"What do I look like without my ratty hat?"

"You have a beard and brown eyes," she said, an edge to her voice and her attention trained straight ahead. "I already told you I don't have trouble recognizing faces."

"Then you won't mind if I shave and buy myself a new hat."

She laughed again, that too-high mirth with a touch of wildness to it. "Fine. Do as you please!"

"Fine. I will." He strode past her, nose tipped in the air.

He did not make it two steps before she lunged and caught his elbow. Fear clouded her expression, her wide blue eyes fixed upon him, her breath too quick and feather-light.

For a long moment they stood frozen in the street, staring at one another.

Then, "Please don't," she whispered, stricken.

"Leonie," he began, but she shook her head, tears building.

"Please, *don't*. I won't know you. I know your voice and your walk and how you fiddle with the lock of hair behind your ear when you're thinking. But the hat . . . is my cue . . . from farther away . . . and the beard . . ." Her tears tumbled and the rest of her words caught in her throat, her whole body trembling.

Thorben tugged her into his arms, enfolding her in a solid embrace. "You little idiot, why didn't you tell me?"

"Tell you?" she echoed, half an octave too high. "Tell you that everyone in a crowd looks exactly the same to me at first glance? That I sometimes can't tell women from men except by the clothes they wear? That I have to catalogue people by the tiniest differences and then somehow *remember*? I knew my own father only by his voice and his smell, and even that wasn't foolproof! I might as well be blind!"

"Blindness would be much worse, Leonie," he said, a knot loosening around his heart. He rubbed a soothing hand on her back.

She clung to his lapels, glaring up at him. "Would it? No one would get offended when I didn't recognize them if I were blind. I wouldn't have to smile and nod at people who refused to identify themselves because I should already know who they are. No one would lecture me about not trying hard enough to remember which face belongs with which title."

He thumbed a tear from her cheek. "No wonder you hated all your suitors."

Another wild laugh erupted from her. "I had a hard enough time in Felstark, with servants and nobles I've known all my life. Can you imagine me having to move to a new house, a new city, a new castle, and start all over again? And how soon would my new husband tire of his precious trophy failing to remember everyone?

My father always thought I was being careless or intentionally rude. He still believes it."

"Shame on him," said Thorben. "You can't assume that everyone would be so callous."

Grudgingly she nodded. "Simon understood. Naira always wore the same brooch on her collar so I could know her at a glance, and Gitta had that glorious red hair that she kept uncovered, but they were the only ones who tried. That wretched Amelise of Rotholt would wear lavender scent one day and rosewater the next, and she changed clothes multiple times in an afternoon, until the only distinguishing feature I could discern was her shrill cackle whenever my father said something even remotely clever."

The spots of pink on her cheeks redoubled in her indignation. He wanted more than anything to kiss her here in the street. "But haven't you done everything you were afraid of? You've moved to a new house, a new city—a new castle, even."

"And I can't tell the head cook from a kitchen runner except when he's talking, and you're set on an annulment so I'll be forced to move somewhere else soon enough."

"Maybe to a convent," Thorben said with mock-solemnity.

A shudder coursed through her. She rested her head on his chest with a huff. "Don't joke. The nuns all look the same *on purpose*. Living there would be an endless nightmare of never knowing who I was talking to."

He tightened his arms around her, resting his chin on her head. "What if I have to shave my beard?"

"Just don't. I don't mind it or your ratty hat."

"But *what if*?"

She grew still. Haltingly, she said, "If, for some reason, you had to, could you be patient? Even a voice or a posture can be unfamiliar if I meet someone where I'm not expecting them."

"I think I can manage that."

She tipped her chin up, eyes shimmering. "So you won't push for the annulment?"

Grimness settled upon him. "That decision, I have been informed, is entirely in your hands."

A sigh of relief heaved from her lungs. "Then abandon any hopes you had for it," she said, snuggling deeper against him.

"You probably want to reserve that judgment." He swallowed, contemplating how—or whether—to disclose his identity. A cowardly voice whispered that he could pretend to leave, to travel for the week of the coronation, return to the castle clean-shaven, receive his crown, and then grow his beard again to resume his life as her beggar husband indefinitely. She would not recognize him from afar, and servants never spoke to their king without being bidden.

He didn't want to live alongside her in a hovel, though. He wanted her beside him on the throne of Hauke.

A throne and a crown she scorned. Would she accept it, or was half his allure his beggar's status, which compelled her to recognize no one other than him?

He couldn't put off his confession any longer.

"Leonie," he said, "there's something you have to know."

She froze for a breath. Then, "If it's your reason for wanting the annulment, the thing that's going to make me hate you, I don't want to hear it."

He huffed. "That's not really a choice."

"Of course it is. I never would have told you my secret if you hadn't guessed it—if you hadn't used it to *threaten* me." She punctuated this with a pinch on his arm. He hissed and jerked away. "You don't have to tell me everything."

"This thing I do. It'll catch up with us."

"Did you murder someone?" she asked, an eager light leaping to her eyes.

"What? No. Why would you jump straight to that?"

"Well, it's obviously some crime if it's going to catch up. Are you a wanted man across the Twelve Kingdoms?"

"Stop. I'm serious right now. You might really hate me."

"Then don't tell me!"

"I have to. But bear in mind: that night your father forced us to marry, I didn't mean to show up on the castle doorstep. I'd have rather been anywhere but there. It was just that the storm—"

A call from further up the street rang out. He paused, frowning. Riders galloped from the castle gates, headed straight for them.

Thorben swore under his breath. Those were his guards. Surely they had not recognized him this far away from the walls. Leonie, glancing that direction, hissed an inhale.

"What do you think they want?"

"We're about to find out." They couldn't outrun eight men on horses, certainly not through this part of the city with its broader avenues and well-spaced buildings. He and Leonie stepped apart, hands clasped and fingers interlaced, as the guards clattered into a circle around them.

Thorben cagily looked up at the captain, who met his gaze with a trace of apology. No greeting or title fell from the man's lips. Only, "The queen has ordered that we bring you to her."

"I don't want to go," said Leonie stiffly. "I've done as she's asked. She can't make me do more than that."

The captain ducked his head. "Begging your pardon, miss, but we weren't sent for you." He shifted his attention back to Thorben. "Please don't fight. I have orders to arrest you if you resist."

"Manacles and all?" the beggar king asked. He dropped Leonie's hands to present his wrists.

As four guards dismounted, she cut in front of him. "You can't take him. He's my husband."

"You're going to find yourself married to the King of Hauke before the week's out," the captain wryly said, and he winked at Thorben.

"I would sooner die," Leonie uttered.

Thorben fought the urge to curse. How could he possibly disclose the truth now? And how were his own guards privy to the secret, that they could sling such a double meaning? Bert must have spilled his guts at last. "Leonie, go home, or come beg a bed at the castle. I can't deny an audience with the queen."

"It would be a most unwise thing to do," his captain sagely agreed.

She looked between them, a furrow cutting her brows. With an irritated growl, she grasped Thorben's hand and staunchly stood beside him. "You can take us both to the queen."

The captain shook his head. "She only wants him. You're welcome to come as far as the gates, but you'll have to part ways there."

Her grip tightened. Thorben was going to wring his mother's neck.

They marched, four guards on foot around the couple and another four on horseback, up to the castle gates and straight through. It was not the homecoming Thorben had expected when he left half a month before, but at least the evening shadows obscured him from any curious onlookers. When the path split, the guards paused. The captain sent a significant glance toward Leonie, nodding his chin the direction that would take her to the servants' quarters.

Thorben squeezed her hand. "I'll see you soon."

Impulsively she kissed his cheek. "I'm going to yell at her," she whispered.

"Oh, you definitely shouldn't," he said, shaking his head. "No one yells at the Queen of Hauke."

"I can't tell her apart from a peasant, so I don't care."

He almost laughed—would've outright guffawed if her intention hadn't lain with enraging his mother. The guards separated them, though reluctantly, and ushered Thorben toward the castle's main entrance. A final glance over his shoulder revealed Leonie still at that split in the path, watching him until the very last moment when he would vanish from her sight.

The last moment she would positively know which man he was among the group.

He absolutely loved the fierce and contrary princess. His heart nearly burst from his ribcage on the realization. Two minutes more, and he might have determined whether she could love him as well.

As he passed beneath the pointed stone arch into the entrance hall, he shifted his attention to the captain that led them. "I suppose you're having fun."

"It has been quite entertaining, Your Majesty. Please remember that we're acting on the queen's orders rather than our own whims, however."

"I'll remember," Thorben said with a grunt.

CHAPTER 15

Queen Julika of Hauke waited in her private receiving room, away from eyes and ears of servants and courtiers alike. Thorben crossed the threshold, glowering, trusting his anger to stave off his instinctive panic and guilt.

His mother pretended to be wholly engrossed with a huge flower arrangement, shifting blossoms from one side to another, ignoring his presence until the door snicked shut behind him.

Only then did she look up, her expression entirely languid. Their eyes locked for a long moment, until she clicked her tongue against her teeth and returned to arranging flowers.

"I beg your pardon," Thorben said in rising indignation.

"As you should," said the queen with a lightness that contradicted her words. "I gave you leave to visit a neighboring kingdom and hunt with friends, not to marry on the sly and masquerade as a beggar in your own capital."

He snapped his mouth shut, no ready answer to this statement. The silk of her royal blue gown rustled as she circled the overflowing vase. "Besides that, you should have been home three days ago. Your coronation garments still need their final fittings, and foreign guests are starting to arrive and expect to greet the new king." She removed a sprig of white lilies and repositioned them ninety degrees to the left.

Thorben, sulking, buried his hands in his pockets and slouched further into the room. "Bert told you everything?"

"I haven't spoken with him. I'd rather not know how much he knew."

"Then how—?"

"I received a letter from the Duke of Ursinbau, dated the morning after your accidental union. I then quizzed your valet who was commanded to visit his family, and finally I sat Marco down and explained that until the crown rests officially on your head, he is accountable to *me*. I *might* have given you another day or two, but when you decided to canoodle almost on my very doorstep, I figured that tonight was as good as any to pull you in."

His bravado deserted him on a heavy sigh. He dropped into the nearest chair and buried his face in his palms.

She had known all along. Why had he not considered that Ursinbau might betray him to his mother? And Gereon, and Marco—!

"The beard has to go, Tor," the queen abruptly said. "You're an eyesore in general, but that is the worst offense. You're not getting crowned with that scraggly mess on your face."

"Have you just been toying with me?" he asked.

Her brows arched, aloofness in her expression. "I thought I was allowing you some autonomy. You didn't use it very wisely, but I suspect spending time as a beggar has enlightened you in more ways than you realize."

The poverty of Swifthaven's lower wards pressed upon him, squalor he had never imagined could exist. He foresaw many a meeting with his council about how to address the multitude of problems he had encountered there. That would necessarily wait until after his coronation, though. More pressingly, "What about Leonie?"

"Ursinbau seemed to think you two would suit, if you could get past your initial aversion to one another."

A cynical laugh cut from him. He ran a hand down his face, suddenly exhausted.

His mother regarded him for a long, silent moment, hands demurely clasped in front of her. Then, "Why haven't you told her who you are?"

"I was about to, but a squad of guards interrupted us."

She hummed in mock sympathy. "I'm sure that was the first opportunity that presented itself."

He suppressed an urge to growl, too aware of how accurate her observation was. "If you had a letter from Ursinbau, you must know I wanted my identity kept secret. And if you've known where I was all along, why didn't you push for the annulment Marco was requesting on my behalf?"

She blinked. "Why should I want the marriage annulled? Up until that idiot Prince of Arbenia showed up, I was content to let the annulment happen, if that's what you both chose, but I certainly wasn't going to advocate for it. I'm the one who sent you to Felstark in the first place, remember?"

"But you didn't expect this outcome," Thorben said. "You couldn't."

"I wouldn't have sent you if I objected to it." She allowed the full import of her meaning to settle on him, then she waved a dismissive hand. "Leonie of Elisia was such a sweet, shy girl." He scoffed; she ignored the interruption. "Obviously you two didn't care a whit about one another when you met as children, but that didn't mean you might not get along well enough as adults."

"She intends to yell at you for arresting her beggar husband."

A glint of satisfaction flashed in his mother's eyes. "I look forward to it."

No doubt she did. Queen Julika had always carried a strange sense of humor, especially towards those who dared speak their passions aloud to her.

Thorben, resigned to the impending confrontation, asked, "Are you going to tell her who I am?"

"And rob you of that penance? No, I don't think so."

His stomach churned. "She'll want the annulment when she learns the truth."

"So be it. You can't live a double life as a beggar and a king."

This bloodless truth struck him like a cudgel in the gut. He returned his face to his palms, digging his fingers into his hair. Fabric rustled, and the deep blue of his mother's dress slid into his periphery. A light hand settled atop his head.

"Gereon's in your room drawing you a bath, ready and waiting to restore you to your rightful form. I'll have dinner sent up. You can sleep in a proper bed tonight and see how you feel in the morning."

"What about Leonie?" he hoarsely asked again.

"She can have any bed in the castle that she wants. Until she knows the truth, you can't be seen together. If she decides against an annulment, you'll have to get married again anyway." When he looked up in surprise, she tutted. "Really, a secret kitchen wedding for the King of Hauke? It will never do. You'll have an appropriate betrothal period, with time to court as needed. *If* she agrees to keep you, Tor."

He swallowed against a sudden lump in his throat. "And if she doesn't?"

The queen tipped her head, eyes distant as she considered. "Hauke would have to settle a handsome sum on her for the insult of our king's trickery, enough that she could live comfortably wherever she pleases. Roughly the same amount, I imagine, that we would pay for a royal wedding, which means that you would of necessity remain single for several more years while we rebuilt that particular fund."

Ruefully he shook his head. "That I can live with."

She lightly flicked his temple. "Go to your room, my silly son. You're exhausted." As he rose, she squeezed his hand, a reassuring smile upon her lips.

"I am sorry," Thorben said.

"Are you? I should think you would wait until this all resolved before deciding that."

A blush climbed his neck. "No, I mean I'm sorry for worrying you."

His mother cradled his cheek in her palm, eyes dancing. "I wasn't worried, just annoyed." Then she patted his face and sent him on his way. He crossed into the hall in a daze, feeling like a child who had played outside longer than he was supposed to.

———

Guards escorted him to the castle's residential wing, careful to avoid encounters with any visiting nobles and dignitaries along the way. His royal apartment seemed astronomically large after two weeks in a meager hut. He stared in wonder at a ceiling so high that he might stand on another man's shoulders and still not reach it.

The bed alone would have filled his beggar's hovel nearly wall to wall. It seemed almost criminal even to contemplate sleeping in it.

His valet greeted him with a dubious once-over and a disapproving sniff. Thorben shed his tattered clothes, which Gereon confiscated for instant destruction. The hot water of his bath embraced him in its depths, easing his muscles and allowing his thoughts to roam free.

Where was Leonie? Had she claimed her rank to gain access to the queen, or had she accepted a bed in the servants' dormitory?

More importantly, would she ever forgive him? He might have told her the truth a thousand times, but pride had always stilled his tongue. Was it worth it, engaging all these tangled emotions? Fear and adoration mingled freely within him.

She despised Thorben of Hauke not for himself but because of what he represented: a new life, a horde of unknown faces and mannerisms, the anxiety of standing alone in a sea of perpetual strangers, never knowing when one might take offense where none was intended.

Everything about her suddenly made sense—even *Thrushbeard,* which shared its syllable beginnings with how she had been taught to pronounce his name. She had catalogued him by a distinguishing feature, his cleft chin, and simply added a label to help her remember name and face together.

That clever, vicious, adorable woman!

He left water noticeably more clouded than it had been when he entered the bath, every inch of his skin scrubbed clean. His dimpled chin reappeared under Gereon's masterful handling of a razor. Thorben was almost sad to see the beard go, but the face that stared back at him in the mirror was his own once again.

It was a face Leonie would not readily recognize, and certainly not as her husband's if she did.

When, clad in fine clothing, he tried to leave his apartment again, he discovered a pair of guards outside his door.

"Your mother wishes you to rest tonight," one said.

Doubtless they had orders for what to do if he refused. "Where's Leonie? Is she with the queen?"

"The young lady did request an audience, but Her Majesty's secretary has informed her that the queen only meets with commoners at the start of each week. The young lady declined to claim any other standing and is housed in the women's dormitory for the evening."

So his mother and his wife were locked in a battle of wills. That did not bode well for future relationships. "I want to see her."

"Men aren't allowed in the women's dormitory," said the second guard, deadpan.

"I suppose we could invite her to your room," said the first with a speculative glance to his fellow, "but that would likely raise eyebrows in the servants' quarters."

Thorben winced. A king summoning a beautiful kitchen maid to his private apartments late in the evening would give all the wrong impressions to anyone who heard the story. Besides, Leonie would reject such a summons out of hand.

"I hate you both," he told the guards.

They merely grinned. He retreated back into his rooms and shut the door.

CHAPTER 16

Thorben meant to seek Leonie out first thing in the morning, but he awoke to the royal tailor entering his bedroom, with half a dozen attendants all carrying garments that needed final fittings. Thorben blearily submitted, answering questions mostly in grunts as he raised and lowered his arms on command.

"You're leaner than you were a month ago," the tailor observed, pinning gold-embroidered material for a better fit around his king's torso. "Was the hunting in Elisia not as prosperous as expected?"

"I caught everything I could possibly want from there," Thorben said.

Would the creature who had caught him want him in return, though? Was she in the kitchens today, or had she asserted her status to demand an audience with the queen?

Had she heard that the ascendant king had returned sometime during the night?

When at last the fitting ended, Gereon fussed over him like a mother cat grooming one of her young. Thorben emerged from his apartment at last looking every bit like royalty, from the carefully arranged hair to the immaculately tailored jacket and breeches, and the shining, spotless boots that hugged his calves as though molded to them.

He made it only a dozen yards before dignitaries beset him, offering their greetings and congratulations. All too soon, his cheeks ached from too much diplomatic smiling. Somehow he ended up in the dining hall, where breakfast adorned the table. Every gray-clad servant made him start, but none had the sunshine-colored hair he sought. He endured compliments and salutations, hugs from his little sisters, stories of the roads between Swifthaven and half a dozen other kingdoms.

When Alois of Arbenia appeared, he finally despaired of seeking Leonie.

"Thrushbeard, old boy, where the devil have you been?"

Awkward laughter met this ostentatious address, eyes sliding toward the young king to see how he accepted the ill-gotten nickname.

"I went hunting, dullard," Thorben replied in a lighthearted voice.

Alois scowled, and even more so at the chuckles that erupted around him. He leaned in, lowering his voice. "I don't appreciate that particular nickname, Tor."

The king blandly smiled. "Do tell." He allowed the mild remark to sink in, a process which took longer than it should have. Leonie had certainly assessed Alois well when she renamed him.

A ruddy hue rose upon the Prince of Arbenia's cheeks. "Understood," he said, his voice clipped.

Not wishing to incur a grudge, Thorben said, "I'm glad. What brings you to Swifthaven? I didn't expect you at my coronation, did I?"

Alois shifted his stance, eyes flitting to the corner of the dining room. "Something of mine was stolen in Felstark, and I was able to trace it here. I'm still searching for the blackguard who took it from me."

Ice shot through Thorben's veins, every last shred of his self-restraint required not to lunge at the other man. "Something important? Can I help you in your search?"

"Oh, no. It's important to me but a trifling matter to anyone else. I wouldn't want to trouble you, especially with your coronation imminent. Don't worry on my behalf. As soon as I find it, I'll scare off back to my own kingdom again."

"And if you don't find . . . *it*?" Thorben carefully said.

Alois met his gaze and looked away again, clenching his jaw. "I haven't planned that far."

"Well, keep me in the loop. Theft is such an unsettling crime. I should hate for you to be deprived of your property, however trifling it might seem to others."

The prince nodded, far more reserved than he had been when he entered. Thorben itched to punch him, but he affected a pleasant smile instead. When Alois finally left an hour later, he breathed a sigh of relief.

One gathering bled into another as the day wore on. Every attempt he made to escape ended in handshakes and stories from newly arrived guests.

"What did you expect?" his mother asked when he sidled next to her to utter a low complaint. "If you'd been here three days ago, they would have come to you as they arrived. Now everyone needs to greet you at the same time, and you, the ever-gracious host, should accommodate them accordingly."

"The only person I need to accommodate is Leonie."

Queen Julika slid him an amused glance. "The stubborn girl refuses to invoke her title to speak directly to me. I sent her a message assuring her that you were comfortable and that you could see her as soon as you've fulfilled your obligations to the kingdom. Doubtless she interpreted that as a prison sentence."

"This is not funny," Thorben said. "You're not funny at all."

"On the contrary, I am quite entertained. Oh, cheer up, Tor. She'll surely be relieved to see you again at last."

He scowled. "Or enraged."

His mother's chuckle rang upon the air. "I do hope I'm there to witness it. You're both terribly silly children." She moved away from him then, and he realized he was being punished—a punishment he might deserve but Leonie did not.

More nobles arrived throughout the afternoon, and that ongoing reception led into an evening of music and dancing. Thorben, forced to partner with several lovely, doe-eyed young ladies, kept looking for his nearest exit. Alois showed up with Marco, Bert, and the spirited Ilsebeth, all of whom eagerly welcomed their king back to his castle.

He pawned the Prince of Arbenia off on one of the ladies who kept trailing him, favored his advisor with a withering glare, and ignored Bert altogether.

Gray-clad servants brought food and drink for the assembled company, well prepared for an impromptu pre-coronation party. Leonie was not among them, but Thorben noted the inconspicuous curtain through which the help entered and exited the hall. He edged toward it slowly, greeting guests along the way.

"Subtle," Marco said as he slipped by to fetch a fresh drink.

The traitor.

An ambassador from Nikelberg waylaid the young king ten feet from the passageway, eager to convey felicitations from several notable families of that kingdom. When he started into talk of timber mills and flax exports, any hope of escaping his presence fled. Thorben half-listened, nodding or humming at appropriate intervals to signal his attentiveness.

The curtain in his periphery wafted, but no one passed through. He angled his head and his gaze connected with a pair of ocean-blue eyes.

Shock thrummed down his spine. Leonie's focus flitted beyond him to the sparkling company, searching, not a hint of recognition in her guarded expression.

He interrupted the Nikelbergian ambassador. "Excuse me, please. I do beg your pardon." With quickening breath and heart leaping into his throat, he dashed for the curtain.

Leonie, too busy scanning the crowd, did not see him until he was almost upon her. She hissed a sharp inhale and recoiled into the hall. Thorben, intent upon speaking with her at last, swept the curtain aside and followed.

"Leonie, wait!"

She would know his voice, wouldn't she?

But she'd asked for patience for this very reason. Instead of pausing, she ran faster. Thorben caught her wrist halfway down the hallway.

"Let me go!" she shrieked, flailing. He caught her other wrist as she tried to strike him. "I was only looking for the queen. I want nothing to do with you!"

The words stung, but he held her fast, hoping to speak through the haze of frenzy that enveloped her. "Leonie, it's me. You said you could recognize my voice, my posture, my mannerisms. Do you recognize any of it?"

Beneath his searching gaze she froze. The whites of her eyes shone, her horrified attention fixed on him.

A faint laugh shook his frame, the hope that he'd fostered cracking at its edges. "This is it. The reason I said you would hate me, the secret you didn't want to know. I'm not a beggar and I never was."

"Tor," she breathed.

"Thorben," he corrected, "of Hauke."

She shook her head. "No."

"I'm sorry. I wanted the annulment so that I'd never have to tell you."

"No!" She wrenched free of his grip, her back hitting the wall. Instead of scrambling away, she fell to her knees, threading her fingers into her pale hair, eyes unseeing. "This can't be right."

Tentatively he knelt before her, trying to catch her gaze, reaching out as though to comfort but too hesitant to touch her. "I'm sorry, Leonie. I honestly never meant to cross your castle's threshold again. Bert and I went busking on a lark and got lost in the storm on our way back to the embassy. The whole thing was a stroke of bad luck."

"Bad luck?" she echoed, fire flashing through her. She shoved his shoulder. "*Bad luck*? How does that begin—? Oh, Simon *knew*, didn't he? And he just—just—!" Her words stuck in her throat, fury and tears overtaking her.

Thorben's heart sank, his worst fears mushrooming within him. "What did Ursinbau tell you?"

A short, wild laugh burst from her lips. "That this marriage might prove favorable, that I'd only have to keep track of one person, so it wouldn't hurt to try! And all the while he knew who you were, and you were sneering up your sleeves at me—!"

"I never sneered," Thorben said. "We both agreed that we didn't want to marry—"

"But only one of us knew who the other person was! Did you enjoy watching as I failed at everything? And pretending to be poor so I could suffer? And letting me say such terrible things about you to your face?"

His sins piled high before him, an insurmountable wall he had built through his own callous actions. A somber hush possessed him. "No, I didn't enjoy it."

She scoffed.

It would never work. No defense he raised now could change the events of the past. Mouth suddenly dry, he said, "The annulment is yours to command. Hauke will issue you a payment as recompense for my mistakes, and—"

"And you just wash your hands of me," Leonie interjected fiercely, "as though money and a wave goodbye can restore everything back to its proper order. How could I be such a *fool?*" She buried her face in her palms, shuddering against emotions that sought to overpower her.

But why? Wasn't he offering what she wanted? Why would that anger her, unless . . . ?

He sat back on his heels, that spark of hope reigniting. "You don't *have* to choose annulment." She stilled. His heart quickened on this tiny sign that he might still plead his case. "We could stay married. I understand that you don't want to be the Queen of Hauke, but at least you already know something of the patterns here. It wouldn't be such an abrupt transition. And I would help, of course."

Slowly she lifted her head, teary eyes bluer than ever as she examined him. "*You're* not pushing the annulment?"

"I told you, I only wanted it to save face. That's not possible anymore."

"But if this whole charade was to humiliate me—"

"I wasn't trying to humiliate you. I just didn't know how to get out once we were both trapped. If the choice were solely mine—" He caught the rest of his sentence between his teeth. Embarrassed, he glanced at the blank walls of the servants' passage, reluctant to speak his heart aloud to the one person who could dash it into pieces.

"Yes?" Leonie prompted.

At last he tipped his head, looking her straight in the eyes as he submitted to her demand. "I'd keep you forever. Even if you want to call me Thrushbeard for the rest of my days."

For an excruciating breath, the confession hung between them. Then, she seized his shirtfront, crumpling the expensive fabric in her fist as she dragged him forward. Her kiss tasted of salt tears, and never had a sweeter sensation passed his lips. He cradled her, any shyness between them melting in the joy of longing fulfilled at last.

"Please don't call me Thrushbeard," he pled when first he could. "I hate that name so much."

"But you have such a nice, pronounced dimple," she replied, and she kissed the corner of his mouth.

"And don't call me Thorben, either," he said, lisping the first consonant as the people of Elisia always did. "I hate that even more."

She tutted. "You really are a beggar."

A breathy laugh escaped him. "And you're a beggar's wife. Only one of us looks the part right now, though."

"And the other looks like a king philandering with a pretty servant."

He sat back on a huff and wryly said, "You little shrew."

She followed, flinging her arms around his neck. "Yes, and you're stuck with me."

He held her tight, content to remain thus for the foreseeable future. A last confession yet remained, though. He swallowed his instinctive cowardice and spoke.

"Leonie, there's one more thing. That day at the market, when all your pottery was crushed . . ."

She drew back, meeting his gaze, a faint frown tugging at her brows.

"I was the horseman," he sheepishly said. Her breath caught, and he pressed forward. "It was Alois's horse. I saw him meet you, and I followed him. He was planning to come back and carry you off at day's end, so I stole his horse while he was in a pub."

"And you rode it through my stall," the princess said, her voice flat.

Thorben nodded. "To make you go home early. I'm so sorry."

To his surprise, she leaned in and kissed him again. When she drew back, she said, "You owe me a whole new set of dishes."

"They're yours, and anything else you want."

She accepted this penance with a magnanimous incline of her head. "I'll start a list."

"Honestly," said the queen, "trysting in a servants' corridor. You've set the whole castle talking."

"The servants, maybe," Thorben muttered. The multitude of dignitaries and ambassadors were still oblivious to the young couple that would soon reign Hauke together. Since guards had escorted the pair to the queen's private receiving room, the multitude would remain oblivious for the time being, too.

He squeezed Leonie's fingers interlaced with his own, and she spared him a sidelong smile.

His mother, unimpressed, regarded both of them. "Would the Princess of Elisia like to make any requests or demands?"

"Can you banish the dullard?" Leonie asked.

The queen shifted her attention to Thorben for an explanation. "She means Alois."

"I think it best he knows why he's being asked to leave. A competent king should be able to communicate that much."

He huffed a laugh. "Fine. I'll tell him." Alois would take the news hard and he might get ugly about it, but they were in Hauke, so he'd show restraint. Besides, he'd never had a true claim to Leonie anyway. If this damaged the kingdom's future relations with Arbenia, so be it.

Queen Julika shifted her attention back to the princess. "Anything else?"

Leonie edged a degree closer to Thorben. "Perhaps some advice. Am I to write my father?"

"I believe you and your husband might pen a letter of congratulations to him together. I understand he has recently remarried."

"To a pestilence," the princess uttered. After another breath, she stamped one foot in a flouncing movement. "It's like he won, though. He wanted to marry me off to a foreign royal, and he *did*."

The queen shrugged. "Sometimes we have to let our adversaries have their petty victories. No doubt he'll find a frosty reception in Swifthaven should he ever travel here. Though I won't quibble with the outcome, I think we all disapprove of his methods."

Thorben and Leonie exchanged a glance and, in spite of themselves, softly smiled.

"Right," said their audience of one. "Perhaps we could drop the lovesickness a degree. There's still a coronation and a proper

Haukien wedding yet to come. Plenty of time to make eyes at one another where you won't turn your mother's stomach."

"No one's forcing you stay," Thorben said.

Leonie nodded. "It's perfectly fine to leave us together. We had a priest and everything."

Queen Julika rolled her eyes. "Children, both of you." But she strode from the room without a backward glance, thus allowing the couple to resume their quiet tryst.

EPILOGUE

EIGHT MONTHS LATER

It's bad luck for a groom to see his bride before the ceremony, Tor." Ilsebeth, holding the door open only a slit, peered out with disapproval sparking in her eyes.

Thorben merely shrugged. "Then it's bad luck regardless: she and I are walking to the altar together."

The young noblewoman pursed her lips tight. Doubtless she wanted him to wait in the antechamber outside the chapel, but he had no intention of lingering where guests could accost him. Much better to hole up with Leonie until the ceremony was ready to start.

Thus, he arched an eyebrow at the self-appointed guardian of the bridal suite. Although Ilsebeth shook her head, her dark ringlets dancing around her face, she did reluctantly step back to allow him entrance.

"Who is it?" Leonie called from further in the room. Burgundy-clad attendants surrounded her, adjusting the fit of her long sleeves and the hem of her full skirt, arranging the way her veil overlayed her softly curling hair that fell past her gold-beaded waistband.

Thorben fought the instinct to catch his breath at the vision of perfection she posed. " 'Tis I, the King of Hauke, come to pass his future queen's inspection." Pausing halfway between her and the door, he stretched his arms straight and turned in a circle, thereby to exhibit his own wedding finery.

She'd seen it several times before, during fittings, but that didn't stop the corners of her mouth from twitching upward. "Very nice. And mine?" She glanced down to her pale, gold-embroidered gown.

"Stunning—no less than the one who wears it."

True to her nature, Leonie made a face and returned her attention to the mirror. "Did you peek into the chapel?"

"On my way here. It's packed."

"Anyone I should be aware of?"

"Alois came with the Arbenian royals, but he has a pretty damsel hanging on his arm. Marco has sworn to cast him from the city if he makes any fuss whatsoever."

"Sounds like he's moved on to greener pastures," Leonie said as she inspected the beading on one sleeve. "I wish him well."

Thorben fought the urge to laugh. Once Alois had stopped posing a threat to her mental wellbeing, she had abandoned calling him "the dullard." According to Marco, the Arbenian prince had brought a lady from his own court as means of saving face rather than from any genuine interest, but it was a step in the right direction.

"I also wish him well," said the King of Hauke.

Leonie favored him with a small smile then dropped her gaze again. "Any news from Elisia?" She kept her voice light, as though she didn't care about the answer, but the way she fiddled with her fingertips betrayed her.

Thorben cleared his throat. "They're not in the chapel yet, but Ursinbau arrived an hour ago, along with his wife and children. There were some other Elisian nobles in the party too—I think I saw the wine barrel among them."

"The wine barrel . . . ?" she vaguely echoed. Then, "Oh! You must mean Dolbach. How do you remember my terrible nicknames better than I do?"

"Having borne one makes me oversensitive."

Leonie wrinkled her nose. "Yours wasn't so bad. And it's hardly my fault that he's the exact same shape as the casks his vineyard uses." She shifted her attention back to the mirror, pretending to smooth out an invisible crease in her gorgeous skirt. "Simon's the official Felstark Castle representative, then?"

Though she affected aloofness, Thorben could sense her simmering resignation. "You timed this wedding specifically so that your father couldn't come," he gently reminded her.

"I timed it so his *pestilence of a wife* couldn't come," she said with a pout. The expression cleared. "Though, I suppose if he left her alone at this point of her confinement, he'd be a terrible father."

"He's a terrible father regardless."

A grin leapt to her face, with a hint of wickedness to it. "I hope the baby's a strapping, healthy girl, and that she runs him ragged in his old age."

The door into the chamber opened and shut, admitting a young woman in the midnight blue now worn by Swifthaven Castle's ladies' maids. Her flame-red hair, braided beneath a stark white cap, blazed against the darker fabric of her dress. She dropped into a curtsey that was elegant despite the parcel she carried. "Your Highness, I have returned."

"Don't be silly, Gitta," said Leonie. "I've told you a thousand times not to curtsey, and I'd recognize your hair even if you didn't announce yourself."

The Elisian maid, along with her sweetheart—now her husband—had joined Swifthaven Castle within a month of Leonie's advent. The castle uniform with its smaller cap allowed her hair to remain visible despite her marital status, if she so desired, which suited her and Leonie perfectly.

The uniforms themselves had changed as well. After private consultation with the newly ascended king and his affianced, the dowager Queen Julika had arranged for servants to dress according to their area of employ: the original gray garb for the housemaids, beige for the kitchens, green for the gardens, brown for the stables, burgundy for the tailors and laundry, and midnight blue for the personal staff. All colors were muted but distinct enough from one another. Although no one explained a reason for this change, the servants embraced their new branding.

"I wouldn't dare not curtsy, Your Highness," Gitta said, mild reproof in her voice.

Leonie hummed, dissatisfied, but shifted her attention to the parcel in her maid's hands. "What do you have?"

"The Duke of Ursinbau brought your mother's wedding tiara, in the event that you wished to wear it."

The princess froze, her blue eyes wide. Gitta, ignoring this startled reaction, crossed to a small table, there to open the box and reveal its contents. From its depths she removed a sparkling headpiece. When she positioned it in the sunbeams of the nearby window, it scattered tiny rainbows throughout the room.

Leonie's breath hitched. "I'd've thought Amelise would sooner die than let that leave the treasury."

"She has no claim on it." Gitta studiously used her sleeve to polish the central diamond, as though this task required her full attention. "It belonged to *your* mother, not the Elisian Crown. Besides, though His Grace didn't say as much outright, I'm fairly certain your stepmother doesn't know it's missing."

Thorben snorted but quickly covered his mouth. When Leonie shifted her concerned gaze to him, he smiled. "I think you should wear it."

The princess vaguely touched the tiara that already graced her golden hair—a lovely piece on loan from Queen Julika's own collection. "Will your mother mind?"

"Not at all," he said with utmost certainty.

A shimmer in her eyes betrayed the emotions she kept in tight restraint as Gitta carefully removed one tiara and replaced it with the other.

The maid stepped back. "It's perfect."

Leonie laughed, and a tear escaped. Thorben, quick to respond, pressed his handkerchief into her hands. She dabbed at her face, self-conscious in the hush that had fallen across the room.

"Shall we give you two some time alone before the ceremony?" Gitta asked.

"It's bad luck," Ilsebeth hissed beside her.

"They've spent all their bad luck," the maid replied in much the same tones. "Besides, they're already half married." Then she began shooing people from the room. The burgundy-clad attendants, having finished their last adjustments, retreated. Ilsebeth spared the royal couple a final disapproving glance before Gitta pushed her out the door.

As the latch clicked, Thorben stepped close to Leonie, taking both her hands in his. "Half married, and a ceremony within the hour. Now's your last chance to escape."

"Your last chance to be rid of me, you mean," she said, peering up at him.

Since she already knew his heart, he didn't dignify this with any response other than a tightened grip on her fingers.

A furrow appeared between her brows as she studied his face. After a moment, she shook her head. "Nothing but your dimple sticks."

"That's why I have the crest of Hauke pinned to my collar," he lightly said.

Her blue eyes flitted to that unobtrusive ornament. "Does it bother you?"

"No. I like it."

She squeezed his hands. "Not the pin—or not the pin alone. *All* the concessions: having to stand next to me all the time, greeting people by name so I know who they are, making excuses when I look like I've forgotten someone important. Does that bother you?"

"No," he said again. He'd performed those tasks so many times over the past several months that they were almost second nature now. With a hint of a smile, he ducked his head so they were eye to eye. "Leonie, I don't *want* to stand next to anyone else."

"And you don't mind walking with me to the altar?" She had balked at entering the chapel alone, at braving a sea of faces and hoping she approached her rightful groom instead of a random member of the wedding party.

Thorben rather liked the solution they had reached. "The ceremony's for both of us. Why shouldn't we have a grand entrance together?"

She tried to suppress a laugh, but failed. Even so, doubts flashed across her face.

He tipped his chin, as though considering. "I'm sure Ursinbau would walk you up the aisle if we asked him. Or better yet, you can wait at the front of the chapel, and I'll have my mother walk me up the aisle."

"*Stop*," she said through a chortle. Mindful of her veil and tiara, she rested her forehead against his shoulder. Thorben, equally careful, tucked her close, allowing the moment's tranquility to envelop them both.

Soon enough the door would open, someone would summon them to the chapel, hundreds of eyes would rest upon them while they pledged their troths to one another—this time of their own volition. The afternoon would while away in feasts and the evening in dances, with crowds of guests to greet well into the night.

When the tumult faded, though, they would be as they were now, together in quiet companionship.

"I'm glad it was you," Leonie said, barely a whisper. She tipped her head, venturing to meet his gaze.

Thorben smiled, his heart brimming. "Me too. I cannot imagine a better fate."

Next in

ONCE UPON A PRINCE

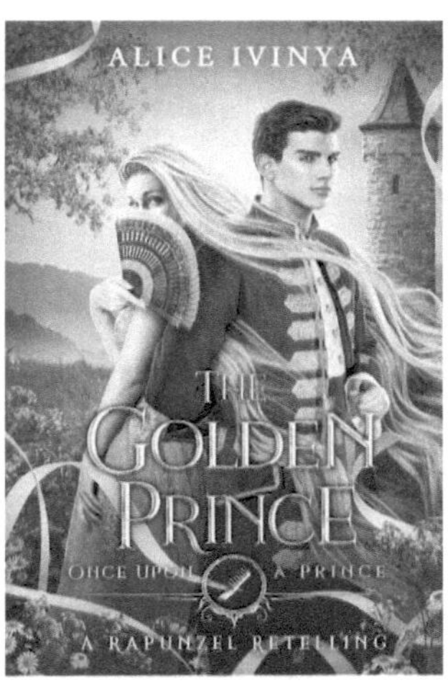

Available October 13th 2023

**A perfect prince. An engagement to save a kingdom.
Too bad it's all a lie.**

Prince Thomas has always been the perfect prince, but now that his kingdom is falling to famine, he must prove his worth and restore the blessing of Spring. All he has to do is find a mysterious woman from a painting and marry her. It's a quest he's been born for. He has everything: the looks, the talent, the perseverance. No matter what peril she is in, he will find and rescue her.

And he'll do so with style.

If Maisie has learned one lesson in her life, it's not to trust anybody. Having been hurt countless times, she lets people see her mask and no deeper. Her practice at deception makes her a master thief, but now she is forgetting which parts of her are real. However, one thing is certain: she does not need any prince to rescue her. In fact, she needs nobody at all.

The hounds of Winter are gathering, leaving death in their wake. The famine is spreading. If Prince Thomas doesn't marry Maisie, the kingdom will fall. But how can he learn to love somebody with a shattered heart?

The Golden Prince, a retelling of Rapunzel, is book 3 of Once Upon A Prince, a multi-author series of clean fairy tale retellings. Each standalone novel features a swoony prince fighting for his happily ever after.

ONCE UPON A PRINCE

The Unlucky Prince by Deborah Grace White

The Beggar Prince by Kate Stradling

The Golden Prince by Alice Ivinya

The Wicked Prince by Celeste Baxendell

The Midnight Prince by Angie Grigaliunas

The Poisoned Prince by Kristin J. Dawson

The Silver Prince by Lyndsey Hall

The Shoeless Prince by Jacque Stevens

The Silent Prince by C. J. Brightley

The Crownless Prince by Selina R. Gonzalez

The Awakened Prince by Alora Carter

The Winter Prince by Constance Lopez

onceuponaprinceseries.com

ACKNOWLEDGMENTS

If you enjoyed this "King Thrushbeard" retelling, you can thank the ONCE UPON A PRINCE series organizers, Constance Lopez and Alora Carter. I never intended to write three incarnations of the same fairy tale, but their invite to a prince-focused multi-author series offered me a new angle of attack.

So naturally, I took it.

Many thanks to Constance and Alora as well for beta-reading the first draft, and to Penny Salisbury, Kristen Ellsworth, Ryan Ellsworth, and Edith Stradling for the same. Your feedback polished this little romp so nicely.

Thank you to MoorBooks Design for the excellent cover, and to Constance and Alora again, because they held my hand and coaxed me through the design process. (And double-thanks here to Constance for being the intermediary. The cover would not be nearly as perfect had I been left to advocate for myself.)

Thanks, too, to the other ONCE UPON A PRINCE series authors: Deborah Grace White, Alice Ivinya, Celeste Baxendell,

Angie Grigaliunas, Kristin J. Dawson, Lyndsey Hall, Jacque Stevens, C. J. Brightley, and Selina R. Gonzalez. This lovely set of peers has been a joy to collaborate with, even though I mostly lurked in the group discussions. Thank you for writing such fun, uplifting, "low spice" stories. Your words are a hope and a refuge.

Thank you, Dear Reader, for allowing me the indulgence of retelling the same story multiple times. I have a writerly obsession with how different a story can be when approached from alternate angles, and this definitely scratched that itch.

Finally, thanks be to God, the Author and Finisher of my faith. My life would be so much more chaotic without His guidance. I am forever grateful.

K.S.
August 2023

ABOUT THE AUTHOR

Kate Stradling is a language-structure fanatic who adores historical and descriptive linguistics. She graduated from Brigham Young University with her BA in English and completed her MA in English at Arizona State. Her published work spreads across the fantasy spectrum, from dystopia lite to fairy tales to kingdom adventures. Devoted to token winters and scorching weather, she lives in sunny Mesa, Arizona.

ALSO BY KATE STRADLING

The Heir and the Spare
The Legendary Inge
Namesake
Deathmark
Goldmayne: A Fairy Tale
Brine and Bone
Soot and Slipper
Maid and Minstrel

The RUSES OF LENORE series
Kingdom of Ruses
Tournament of Ruses
Guardian of Ruses

The ANNALS OF ALTAIR series
A Boy Called Hawk
A Rumor of Real Irish Tea
Oliver Invictus